Bare

JUST THIS ONCE SERIES

NEW YORK TIMES BESTSELLING AUTHOR
DEBORAH BLADON

FIRST ORIGINAL EDITION, MARCH 2018

Copyright © 2018 by Deborah Bladon

All rights reserved. No parts of this book may be reproduced in any form or by any means without written consent from the author.

This is a work of fiction. Names, characters, places and incidents either are the product of the author's imagination or are used factiously. Any resemblance to actual person's, living or dead, events, or locales are entirely coincidental.

ISBN-13: 978-1985447875
ISBN-10: 1985447878
eBook ISBN: 9781926440507

Book & cover design by Wolf & Eagle Media

www.deborahbladon.com

Also by Deborah Bladon

THE OBSESSED SERIES
THE EXPOSED SERIES
THE PULSE SERIES
THE VAIN SERIES
THE RUIN SERIES
IMPULSE
SOLO
THE GONE SERIES
FUSE
THE TRACE SERIES
CHANCE
THE EMBER SERIES
THE RISE SERIES
HAZE
SHIVER
TORN
THE HEAT SERIES
MELT
THE TENSE DUET
SWEAT
TROUBLEMAKER
WORTH
HUSH

Chapter 1

Piper

"Griffin Kent is the worst lover I've ever had." With tears welling in the corners of my eyes, I stare at the woman sitting behind the sleek wooden reception desk. "I can't believe I slept with him. I called the police. They're going to be here any minute."

She looks past me to the frosted glass doors at the entrance of the law offices of Kent & Colt. "If it's a crime to be a dud in bed, my ex-husband would be serving twenty to life right now."

I scrub my hand over my face, mascara staining my palm. "I didn't call them because of that."

"Can I get you a glass of water?" The kind-looking woman is on her feet now. "You look about ready to pass out. Why don't you sit down? We can discuss this."

Discuss what? I went to a hotel with a man last night. We had really bad sex, and when I woke up an hour ago, he was gone along with my wallet and my smartphone.

"I don't want to talk about it." I look beyond her to the massive, exquisitely designed space that obviously houses a number of offices. "Where's the asshole? I need to see him now."

Her lips curl into an unexpected smile. "He's not here. He never gets in until at least nine fifteen."

My gaze drops to my wrist, but the silver watch I always wear isn't there. "He took everything from me."

The middle-aged woman rounds the reception desk until she's next to me, her arm slung over my shoulder. "You listen to me. I don't know what happened between you and Mr. Kent, but there's not a man on the face of this earth who can take everything from a woman."

Great.

I'm in the middle of a crisis and this woman is on her soapbox preaching about the merit of my inner strength.

Griffin Kent took that from me too.

"I don't know what to do," I mutter to myself.

The self-appointed cheerleader next to me adds her two cents even though I didn't ask for it. "You're going to calm down and let me help you. What's your name, dear?"

I feel like I should covet every ounce of personal information after what just happened to me. I was open and trusting when I met the attractive man in the bar last night. I told him my name when he asked. He reciprocated by telling me his. Kent.

An hour later we were in a hotel room and I was proud of myself for checking a one-night stand off my bucket list. I need to wipe that list clean now and focus on one thing and one thing only.

Find some common sense and use it.

"Where are the police? I used the phone at the front desk to call them before I left the hotel. They should be here by now." I stare down at my dress. It's silver shimmer, low cut and much too short to see the light of day. I'd never wear this before nine p.m. and yet, here I am.

Thank the heavens above that my parents are in Denver, completely oblivious to what their only child is doing on her third day in New York City. The move here was supposed to change my life, not drive the entire thing into a ditch at high speed.

"I think we can straighten this out without involving the NYPD."

"How?" I face the woman. She reminds me of my first art teacher in high school. That shouldn't offer me any comfort, but it does. "He needs to be arrested and thrown in jail after what he did to me."

"Were you hurt?" Her eyes scan my face, locking on my green eyes.

I know exactly what I look like. I didn't have time to shower when I crawled out of the hotel room bed, but I did catch a glimpse of myself in the bathroom mirror. My makeup was beyond repair. My shoulder length dark brown hair was such a mess that I used a bright pink hair elastic to tie it up into a tight ponytail.

At least, Griffin Kent left behind my clutch purse with the hair elastic, a tube of lipstick and my apartment keys inside of it.

Either the bastard has a heart, or he overlooked my keys as he was stealing my wallet.

"He didn't hurt me." I fiddle with the business card in my hand. "He took my wallet and my phone when I fell asleep. My watch too. He took it all."

"I find it very hard to believe that Mr. Kent is responsible for this."

Of course, she'd say that. She's the first face anyone sees when they come through the doors of this law office. It's on Madison Avenue. I doubt like hell that her monthly paycheck has less than five zeroes at the end of it. I'd say that's well above the going rate for what blind faith costs in this city.

I shove the business card at her. "I have the proof right here."

She reaches to take the card from me, but I hold tight to the corner of it. It's evidence. He left this behind. I found it on the carpeted floor of the hotel room next to one of my heeled sandals that I'd kicked off before I got into bed with the thieving bastard.

Griffin Kent. Attorney at Law. It's right there in black raised lettering on the card.

If that's not proof, I don't know what is.

"Did he give that to you?"

"He dropped it," I explain. "It must have fallen out of his pocket."

Her tongue skims over her front teeth. "What does Mr. Kent look like?"

I survey the office. There's no movement anywhere. I can hear muffled voices in the distance, but I haven't seen another soul since I walked through the doors to the reception area.

Since the hotel I was at is on Columbus and Eighty-first Street I walked here through Central Park. I spent the bulk of that time rehearsing what I was going to say to Kent once I saw him. I never expected to be subjected to a pre-confrontation interview by his receptionist.

"You know what he looks like," I bite back with a sigh. "I know that he spent the night with me and then robbed me blind."

"Humor me, dear." She squeezes my shoulder. "Describe Mr. Kent to me."

If it's going to take that to chase away the look of doubt that's plastered all over her expression, I'll give her what she wants. "He's the same height as me, blonde hair, full beard, really nice brown eyes."

"What the hell is going on here?" The low rumble of a deeply seductive voice asks from behind me.

"Mr. Kent." The woman next to me turns quickly. "This young woman is here looking for … well, sir, I think I'll let her explain why she's here."

Mr. Kent? The voice I just heard isn't the same one that invited me up to that hotel room last night. I turn around.

Dark brown hair, blue eyes, full lips and a face so handsome that women must stop and stare when he passes them by. I know I would. I can't tear my gaze from him now.

"I'm Griffin Kent," he says smoothly as he nears me. "And you are?"

Chapter 2

Piper

My eyes widen when he offers me his hand. I don't accept because I have no idea what the hell is going on. "You're not Griffin Kent."

His brows arch as he looks at the woman standing next to me before his gaze falls back on my face. "I am Griffin Kent. You're standing in my office, so I'll ask again, who are you?"

I suddenly feel very confused. If he's Griffin Kent who the hell did I spend the night with? I look down at the business card in my hand. It must belong to the tall man standing in front of me in the expensive black suit. He's what I would imagine when I think of an attorney in Manhattan, not the guy who I met last night. That guy was wearing a pair of faded jeans and a brown sweater.

"This young woman found your business card after she was robbed, Mr. Kent." The woman next to me pokes me in the arm as if she needs to clarify which of the three of us she's referring to. "Apparently, she was with a man at a hotel. He took her belongings and left behind your card."

"What did he look like?"

I know the question is directed at me, but I wait for a beat to see if the woman who works for him will keep talking.

She doesn't.

"He had blond hair, brown eyes and he was my height so about five nine." I give my full attention to Griffin Kent now because maybe he knows who the man is. "He had a beard. Men with beards aren't usually my type, but he seemed nice."

Shut the hell up, Piper.

He looks me over from head-to-toe before he points at the business card in my hand. "Is there anything written on the back of that?"

I turn it over to show him. I studied the card on my walk from the hotel. The back is blank.

"I always write my personal cell number on the back of those cards when I give them to clients." His jaw sets. "You found this in a hotel?"

I nod in silence.

"Which hotel?" He digs his cell phone out of his jacket pocket when a chime rings through the air. His gaze skims the screen before he looks back at me. "What's the name of the hotel where you found that card?"

You'd think I'd know that. I could have stored it to memory before I stormed out the door and made my way here. I didn't. I blame my anger for that. It left no room for logical thinking. "I can't remember."

"You can't remember?" he repeats. "I'd say that's a rather important detail in your story."

"Story?" I take a deep breath, pushing back the urge to ask outright if he thinks I made up the experience. Instead, I go for a much more civilized approach. "I just arrived in New York three days ago. I may not recall the hotel's name, but I can tell you exactly where it's located."

That seems to appease him for now. "Did you go to this hotel room with the man in question voluntarily?"

Is this an interrogation? I'm tempted to ask if there's another attorney available who can represent me.

"I did," I answer truthfully without adding the detail that I hesitated briefly when I was in the hotel's elevator because it smelled like old pizza.

"What happened once you got to the room?" he asks matter-of-factly.

Am I supposed to run through the itinerary?
We kissed.
We had sex.
I didn't come.

I opt for a question of my own to save both him and the woman standing next to me the gruesome details of my bad sexual experience. "What do you mean?"

"Did he hurt you or threaten you in any way?" There's not a hint of concern in his voice.

I consider the question. He threatened to fuck me again after he came the first time, but I pretended to be sleepy to save myself the torture of another round of that. "No, it wasn't like that. He didn't hurt me."

"Is this a one-night stand gone wrong?" His eyes give nothing away as he looks into mine.

I take a steadying breath to calm myself before I respond. I know that I don't have to tell him anything, but since he's the only link I have to my missing wallet and phone, I answer. "Yes. We met last night."

He cocks his head as if he's absorbing what I just said. "Joyce will help you sort this out. If I can be of any assistance, she'll let me know."

That's great but who the hell is *Joyce*?

"I should have introduced myself sooner." The woman next to me speaks as if on cue. "I'm Joyce Treadwell, Mr. Kent's assistant. What's your name, dear?"

"Piper," I say softly. "I'm Piper Ellis."

"Good luck with everything, Piper Ellis." A smile eases across Griffin's lips, as he looks me over. "And welcome to New York."

Chapter 3

Griffin

"I hate him and I hired you to make him understand just how deep that hatred runs."

I look across the conference table at Morgan Tresoni. She's attractive if you're into women who spend their days shopping, sipping over-priced cocktails and bashing their almost-ex-husband to anyone who will listen.

I'm paid to listen, so I nod. "I was under the impression that you hired me to represent you in your divorce, Morgan. This is the third time we've been through this process, is it not? You know how this works. You can hate him as much as you want, but you need to remain focused on the bigger picture."

"The bigger picture?" She twirls one of her long red curls around her index finger. "What is the bigger picture, Griffin?"

I look directly into her green eyes. "Your divorce. If you're civil to Marco, this entire process will be over before you know it and you can move on with your life."

"I have moved on," she blurts back with a toss of her hair over her shoulder. "I'm already dating."

I'm not surprised. Morgan has been a regular client for the past few years. She was one of my first appointments when I launched this practice with my friend and college roommate Dylan Colt.

"We're going to meet with Marco and his attorney next week to discuss the settlement." I stress the next sentence with a change in my tone. "Do not leave the country, Morgan. You have to be at that meeting. I don't want a repeat of what happened with Chuck."

The mention of her second husband brings a scowl to her face. "You promised you'd never say his name again. I pay you not to say his name."

The continual reminders of why she pays me grate on my last nerve. "You pay me to keep your bank account well above seven figures. Be available for this meeting, or Marco will come out on top."

She pushes back from the table with exaggerated effort. Unnecessary drama is one of the unfortunate drawbacks of being a divorce attorney. "Fine."

"Stay close to your phone." I stand and button my suit jacket. "I'll have you unattached before you know it."

***

I walk Morgan to the reception area while I listen to her talk about her schedule for the remainder of the day. I don't find any of it interesting, but I say goodbye to her with a smile.

I don't judge the people who hire me. I've never been married so I have no idea how difficult a journey that is. My parents toughed it out for years, but even they couldn't make it to the finish line.

I stand next to the reception desk waiting for Joyce to finish up a call. She was hired on as a receptionist soon after we launched the firm. We wanted someone with a trusting appearance and the ability to calm down emotional clients who stop in looking for a referral.

Since then, Joyce has transitioned into the role of my primary assistant. Today, she just so happens to be filling in for the regular receptionist, Fiona, who is on a two-week vacation that Dylan approved. I was against it initially, but since his dick knows her better than any part of my body ever will, I deferred to him on that.

Joyce ends the call with a promise of a follow-up later in the week. It's an approach that works well when someone is considering leaving his or her spouse. It's free for a caller to chat with the receptionist. They outline the basics to potential clients before I'm brought in for a preliminary consultation.

"Is Mrs. Tresoni behaving herself?" Joyce inches up from her seat to watch Morgan as she leaves through the frosted glass doors.

"Does she ever?" I lean against the reception desk. "Did you take care of the matter from earlier?"

"The matter from earlier?" Her gaze is now locked to a pile of mail. "You're going to need to be more specific. I have a lot going on today, Griffin."

"Piper Ellis." I drag my thoughts back to hours ago when I walked into the office to the sight of a breathtaking brunette in a silver dress. At first, I assumed she was a client who had left her husband after a night of partying and arguing.

I was pleased when I realized that my initial assessment was wrong. Piper Ellis was the victim of a one-night stand gone wrong. It happens. Trusting anyone in this city is a mistake. Piper learned that lesson the hard way.

"Piper," she says her name with a sigh. "That girl is a sweetheart."

"Were you able to track down the man responsible for robbing her?" I ask because my curiosity goes beyond the obvious. Naturally, I'd like to know the identity of the man who left my business card behind, but I'm more concerned with how Piper is doing. It can't be easy putting your trust in someone who fucks you over, both in a literal and figurative sense.

"No." She shakes her head. "We traced her steps back to the hotel she had been at, but there was no sign of that bastard and he paid cash for the room. We did luck out though."

I roll my hand in the air, signaling for her to get to the point.

"One of the hotel employees found her wallet and her phone in the trash in the kitchen. The only thing left in the wallet was her driver's license. Her phone's screen was smashed up pretty good, but she has it back."

"The money and credit cards were cleared out?"

She nods. "Piper said she had left her credit card at home so a small blessing on that front. She had less than fifty dollars in the wallet and the watch she was wearing isn't worth much. Overall, her loss is minimal."

The financial loss she suffered may be restricted to a few dollars and the cost of a replacement phone and watch, but I sense that the blow to her ego and sense of security is substantial.

"Did she make it home alright?"

"We said goodbye at the hotel after she used my phone to call the police to tell them not to bother coming here. She's going to stop at the local precinct and file a report." She lifts her gaze to my face. "I gave her money for cab fare. She said she was going home to change her clothes and then to work."

Work. Again, my curiosity burns so I ask. "Where does she work?"

"She has a job at a place called the Grant Gallery." She flips open the company check pad. "I'm writing myself a check to cover the cab fare to the hotel and back, along with the money I gave Piper. I'll need you to sign this."

"Give yourself an extra hundred for your trouble, Joyce," I say to her surprise. I'm feeling extra generous today. We helped out a damsel in distress. What better way is there to start the week than that?

Chapter 4

Piper

Shit. I am so late. I was supposed to meet Bridget Grant, the co-owner of the Grant Gallery, an hour ago. I tried to call her once I got my phone back from the clerk at the front desk of the hotel. The phone didn't work so after I said goodbye to Joyce I raced home, changed into a red patterned dress and used some of the cash I hid in my freezer to take a cab here.

It was more expensive than the subway, but my livelihood is at stake. Bridget hired me to teach a class at her gallery based on a recommendation from one of my former professors and the samples of my work that I had sent her.

I'm not going to get rich teaching this class, but once I have the schedule worked out, I can take on an extra job to keep a roof over my head.

When I finally walk into the gallery, I'm instantly in love.

It's a stunning space with sunlight filtering in from the street. There are several distinct areas. Sculptures are adjacent to the windows, framed drawings cover the back wall and there's an array of paintings on display near where I'm standing.

I recognize some of them as Brighton Beck originals.

I know that he owns the gallery with Bridget, although she told me on the phone when we first spoke a month ago, that he's not as hands-on with the management as she is.

She's the one who hired me and I'm here to make her proud.

I know what she looks like from the images I've seen of her online. I've followed her work for years. She started out much like I did. She does drawings as well but her tool is a pencil and she hasn't ventured into the realm of nudes.

That's where I shine.

I wave to her from across the gallery. She's standing next to a woman who is staring at a framed drawing of a child with a dog.

I know better than to approach and interrupt. If a potential customer is weighing their decision to purchase, they need room and time to think clearly. Art is a personal investment and it can't be rushed.

Bridget waves back and smiles. She's a beautiful, blue-eyed, petite blonde. She's dressed in a pair of white slacks and a matching blouse. It's an elegant look.

I motion that I'll be near the paintings and she tosses me a nod. I'm grateful that I'll have a few minutes to collect myself before I officially meet my new boss in person.

The past twenty-four hours have been a whirlwind. Being here at the gallery is the highlight of my day, but meeting Griffin Kent runs a close second.

Joyce talked non-stop about her boss as we raced around Manhattan trying to piece my life back together.

He's single. He works too much and according to his assistant, he's never stepped foot in a museum or art gallery.

I'm not surprised. He didn't strike me as the type to find value in anything creative that is meant to bring joy and inspiration to the person who owns it.

He helps people end their marriages. His world is filled with cold destruction.

We have nothing in common, but that hasn't stopped me from thinking about him constantly since I left his office.

As Bridget approaches with the framed drawing of the child with the dog in her hand and the beaming woman by her side, I push all thoughts of Griffin aside.

My new life starts today and that's where all my focus needs to be.

***

"I teach a class on Saturday mornings." Bridget hands me a ceramic mug filled with coffee. "Our studios are upstairs. Beck teaches when he can, but his schedule is all over the place since he's gearing up for a museum showing in Munich."

I'm envious. I know it takes a great deal of talent to reach the level of fame that Brighton Beck has. His watercolor paintings have been displayed in some of the world's most notable museums and galleries and they fetch over six figures at auction.

"Will I get to meet him?" I ask with hope. "I've admired his work for years. Obviously, I've admired your work too."

That lures a subtle smile to her lips. "I promise when he's around, I'll introduce you."

"Have you known him for a long time?" I ask because I don't know the backstory between them. He's been a big deal in the art world for more than a decade. Bridget has emerged as a name in portrait drawings just in the past few years.

"We met at a pub." Her smile stays soft. "I knew who he was instantly. I was in awe but was completely intimidated by him."

I know that I'd feel the very same way. We don't create in the same medium, but I draw inspiration from many different artists.

"He met my best friend that night too," she goes on. "We were both working at the pub. He fell head over heels for her. They got married, he encouraged me to explore my art more and here we are today."

"You never really know what's waiting around the corner," I say quietly.

"That's true." She looks around the gallery. "I never would have imagined that I'd own a place like this and that I'd help new artists learn their craft."

I never thought I'd be offered a job in Manhattan teaching an art class. I'm only twenty-five-years-old. Two weeks ago I was still working at a community center in Denver teaching drawing to whoever wandered in from the street.

"I'm eager to get started, Bridget." I grin. "This is my dream come true."

"You're incredibly talented." She looks up as the door to the gallery opens and a middle-aged man walks in. "He was in yesterday looking at a sculpture. I'll go help him, but consider this job a step toward your future. You're going places. I can sense it."

Teaching at this gallery is going to change my life. I feel it.

Chapter 5

Piper

"Your class will be in the evening." Bridget skims her fingertips over the screen of the tablet in her hands as she sits back down after helping the customer purchase a small sculpture. "We have three other teachers besides you and I. Most of them work Saturdays. I'll introduce you to them at our next staff dinner."

I'm surprised to hear there's a gathering for staff. I'm excited too. I don't know anyone in this city, so I'm eager to meet people who share the same interests that I do. If they are art teachers, I know that we'll at least have that in common. "The staff dinner sounds fun."

"It's a potluck." She looks up from the tablet at me. "We have it at my house on a Sunday afternoon every couple of months. It's very casual. You can bring a plus one and hang out for as long as you want."

I don't bother to mention the fact that I don't have anyone to bring. Bridget knows that I'm new to the city. On the phone when we were discussing the position I told her that I was eager for a new adventure.

I got that, and more, during the past twenty-four hours.

"I've set you up for Monday and Wednesday evenings." She points out the dates on a calendar app on her tablet. "We've had a lot of interest in your class. It's almost full already."

"People are signing up to take my class?" The words sound foreign coming from my lips. "You're sure they know that you're not teaching the class?"

"I'm sure," she answers with a laugh. "There's a page on the studio website devoted to your work. Your students know what you're creating, Piper. Your drawings are captivating. I'm tempted to sit in on a class or two for pointers."

"You?" I raise both brows. "You're not serious? You're Bridget Grant."

"Bridget Beckett." She looks down at her wedding ring. "Grant is for professional purposes. The point is that I've always wanted to feel confident enough to draw nudes, but I don't. If you can teach me how to do it, I'll be in your debt."

"This day has been surreal. I feel like I'm living someone else's life."

"Are you talking about more than just your job here at the gallery?" She brushes her hand over mine. "I'm not a stickler on time, but you were late getting here. I know the city can be complicated to navigate if you're new here. I also noticed your cell phone's screen is cracked. Did that happen today?"

I draw in a quick breath to steady my voice. "I was robbed last night."

"What?" Her gaze darts over my face. "Are you okay? What happened?"

I'm not going to retell the tale of my one-night stand from hell. My boss doesn't need to know about that. I shorten the story to only include the important details. "My wallet and phone were stolen. They were recovered this morning in midtown. My money was gone and my phone's screen didn't survive."

"What a horrible introduction to New York." Her voice is sympathetic. "If you need anything, let me know. I can advance you some money against your first paycheck if that helps and I have an old phone in my desk in the office. You're welcome to use it if you need to."

I'm touched that she's so willing to help me out. "Thank you for the offer, but I have some savings and I'll stop on my way home to get a new phone."

"Don't let that one bad experience taint you, Piper. This is an amazing city. I know you won't regret moving here."

I hope she's right. I bet everything on this move and the last thing I want is to crawl back to my parents' home in Denver to listen to a chorus of I-told-you-so from my dad.

***

"You're 4B?" A woman's voice cuts through the silence of the corridor. "I'm 4A."

I turn to look at my neighbor. I rented this apartment because it's cheap. I wanted to live closer to the gallery but I couldn't afford anything within a twenty-block radius. I may have splurged on a cab to get me there today, but I walked home.

It took almost two hours but it gave me a much clearer picture of the city including the inside of a smartphone store and a police station where I filed a report. The officer on duty at the front desk told me that the chances of catching the jerk that robbed me are slim to none. I thanked him for his time and then stepped back onto the sidewalk of the city I'm now calling home.

Tomorrow I'll purchase a metro card so I can ride the subway to work and save my feet for shorter trips to the bodega and the vintage bookstore down the street.

"I'm Piper." I extend my hand to her even though it's sweaty and clammy from my hike back here. "It's good to meet you."

"I'm Jo." Her long brown hair bounces around her shoulders. "Welcome to the building."

She's older than me by at least two decades. I can tell by the subtle lines around her eyes and the few strands of gray hair that frame her face.

"Do you live alone?"

My eyebrows dart up at her question. I've already been lured into feeling safe by one criminal in the past twenty-four hours, I don't want to willingly walk into another situation where I'll end up losing not only money but my pride.

She giggles. "That was forward of me, wasn't it? I was just asking because I live alone and sometimes it's good for us singles to watch out for each other. Do you know what I mean?"

I relax my shoulders. "I'll keep an eye out for you if you do the same for me."

"You've got yourself a deal, Piper." She holds out her hand in a fist.

I bump mine against it. "It's a deal, Jo."

Chapter 6

Griffin

I stalk down the corridor in the courthouse toward the open elevator. I've already called out once for the people onboard to hold it, but they don't fucking care. Everyone is in a rush to get somewhere in this town and they don't give a shit who they piss off to get there.

Today it's me. As I near the elevator the doors slide shut.

I don't bother reaching in to hold them open because I don't want to ride down with those inconsiderate assholes.

I'll wait for another bunch in the next car and I'll take the trip to the ground floor with them.

"Griffin?"

I don't turn around because I recognize the voice of the person calling my name.

"Griffin? I know it's you."

Of course she knows it's me. I fucked her two months ago, and once a few weeks before that. I really have to start following my rule of no sex with colleagues.

I hear the click-clack of her sky-high heels as she closes the distance between us. I need the elevator to haul ass back up here now.

"Are you avoiding me?" Lana Dunstrom puts her hand on my shoulder. "Why does it feel like you're ignoring me?"

Because I am?

The fuck was fun, but that's all it was. If I wanted a relationship it sure as hell wouldn't happen with someone who I regularly face in court.

I can't wrap my brain around the vision of fucking a woman after we wake up in the same bed and then fucking her over in court a few hours later.

I have boundaries. One of them happens to be that I won't get more involved than a casual screw with a woman I see inside a courtroom.

"I've been busy, Lana." I look down at her. "You've been busy too, I hope. We're due in court the week after next to argue the Lindel case. I take it your client is ready for that?"

She eyes me up with her baby blues. "Mr. Lindel is more than ready to take you on."

I highly doubt it.

He's a coke-snorting, cheating bastard who left his wife home alone for an entire weekend with their three young children while he partied in Southampton like he was single.

"We'll see about that," I say in a low tone. "Your case is weak. Our offer is still on the table. I'll refresh in the event that you've forgotten. My client wants full custody of the kids. Child support, alimony and the deed on the apartment in the city are acceptable. He can keep his party pad in Southampton and his new friends."

"You're dreaming." She runs her hand through her long blonde hair. "What are you doing tonight?"

"Sleeping." I jab my finger into the elevator call button again.

"We can do that together," she purrs.

"I prefer to sleep alone."

She sighs. It's most likely meant to sound breathy and sensual, but it comes across as desperate and dramatic. "I miss you, Griffin. There's no reason why we can't spend another night together."

There are a million reasons why we can't, in the form of dollar bills. I want those to go to Mrs. Lindel. I'm not about to risk the case over a conflict of interest because my cock is involved with the opposing counsel.

I finally turn to face her. "We need to keep our pants on, Lana. This case is a big one. You know your boss would be pissed if he knew you fucked me two weeks before we're in front of the judge."

"How would he find out?"

It's a good question that I have an answer to. "He's walking toward us right now. Put on your game face, sweetheart. You know he plays by the rule book."

She nods and straightens her stance. "I'll see you in court, Mr. Kent. You better be ready for the fight of your life. I'm bringing my big guns."

I step forward when the elevator doors finally open.

Big guns indeed. Her tits are something else, along with the rest of her.

I had a taste but she wasn't for me. I'm looking for something taller and brunette that apparently can be found at an art gallery uptown.

***

I walk into Grant Gallery expecting to see Piper Ellis.

I don't.

Instead, I see a cute blonde talking to an older guy. They seem immersed in a discussion about a painting. From my vantage point, it looks like someone threw a few buckets of paint against a canvas and called it a day.

The colors are muted and subtle. If there's an intentional design to the thing, I can't see it.

I look to my left at a series of sculptures displayed next to the window that faces the street. Again, I'm the wrong person to be judging the value of the pieces. I walk closer to them and realize that someone thinks they're worth more than most new cars. The price tags are staggering.

"I'm Bridget Grant." The blonde is next to me. "Is there something I can help you with?"

I look over her head to where the man is still standing in front of the watercolor painting. "I can wait if you're busy."

"He's considering his options." She smiles softly. "Is there a particular sculpture that you're interested in?"

I turn my back to the pieces of art and face her directly, so there's no misinterpretation. "I'm not here for the sculptures. I'm looking for Piper Ellis."

She looks over at her customer before she turns her attention back to me. "Piper's classes begin the week after next. There's a signup form on our website or I can take care of the registration for you now."

The older guy starts his approach toward us so I finish up our conversation. "Thanks for your time. I'll check out the website."

It's a lie. Piper may be the most beautiful woman I've ever met, but I'm not about to enroll in an art class just to get laid. I'll find another way to connect with the stunning brunette.

Chapter 7

Piper

I look at my new watch. I've been here for a little more than two hours, but it feels like twelve. I've only ever had to do this twice before and both of those times, I had a professor next to me to guide me through the process.

I'm on my own this time. I'm the one teaching the art class, so it's up to me to prepare everything associated with it.

That includes finding nude models.

You'd think the interview process would be fun.

It's not.

I've seen more pictures of naked cocks and breasts this evening than I care to remember.

Right now, I'm trying not to make eye contact with a man who is hotter than most nude models I've ever come across. That's not surprising since his most recent day job consists of modeling for a newly launched underwear line.

"I'll need you for three hours two evenings a week, Rufus." I look over his impressive portfolio on the tablet in front of me. He emailed me the link after the resource center at a local art school sent me his details.

They had a list of models that had posed for classes in the past. I need a model. It was Bridget who suggested I contact them since she has found a few portrait models through them.

"Does the pay I quoted in the email work for you?" I finally look up at his face.

"It works." He flashes me a killer smile.

"I have a standard contract for you to look over and if you're comfortable with it, we can start next Monday."

"Monday works and I'll sign anything you need me to. I'm saving for a vacation in Hawaii."

I instantly picture a nude beach with dozens of muscular blue-eyed, blond-haired men that look like him playing volleyball.

"You're free to go," I say with a grin.

"Cool." He stands and extends a hand toward me. "It was good to meet you, Piper. I think we'll work well together."

I shake his hand. Since he'll be frozen in place while I'm guiding my students on the finer points of drawing the human form, he's probably right. We will work well together if he can stay still and not flirt with every woman in the class.

"So, I'll catch you on Monday?" he asks as he shoulders the navy blue backpack he brought with him. "You'll email me the contract before then?"

"Monday it is and I'll email the contract to you tomorrow."

"I'm stoked." He looks around the almost empty room that I'll transform into a studio for students. "I think we're going to make magic in here."

Bare   *Deborah Bladon*

That's wishful thinking. All I'm hoping for is that a group of people will show up with a passion for art that runs as deep as mine.

***

Until now, I haven't understood the appeal of man in a three-piece suit. Specifically, a man in a gray three-piece suit with a black dress shirt and a gray patterned tie.

I've never been attracted to corporate types. All of the men I've been involved with have had a passion for creativity. I always believed that the pull toward them stemmed from our mutual interest in the arts or their laid-back style.

Griffin Kent has neither of those, but I can't take my eyes off of him.

He's standing near an open office door talking to a woman with long black hair. Her back is to me and his eyes are pinned to her face. A twinge of envy rolls through me. I wish to hell he was looking at me with the same intensity in his gaze.

My sole purpose when I came to the offices of Kent & Colt today was to return the forty dollars that Griffin's assistant, Joyce, loaned me.

Since no one is at the reception desk, I've been standing next to it, eyeing up Griffin since he stepped out of one of the offices with the dark-haired woman. He has yet to notice me staring at him. I'm grateful for that.

I thought I'd hand Joyce the cash and be out of here in thirty seconds flat. That's why I'm wearing ripped jeans, a gray University of Denver T-shirt and a wrinkled black blazer I found at the bottom of my suitcase as I was unpacking more of my stuff this morning.

At least I straightened my hair and brushed my teeth.

My plan today was to stay home so I could work on the lesson plan for my class. When my dad called me an hour ago to ask if I was still alive and if I needed any cash to make ends meet, it dawned on me that I hadn't paid Joyce back.

I was dressed and on the subway within fifteen minutes headed here.

I now wish I had used the number she gave me and called her before I left my place. If I had done that, I wouldn't be standing here looking like a lost puppy.

My gaze scans the reception desk for an envelope. If I can find one, I'll shove the two twenty dollar bills inside and address it to Joyce from me. She'll know exactly what it is.

"If you tell me what you're looking for, I'll point you in the right direction."

There's no mistaking that deep, raspy voice. I know exactly who it belongs to. I look up to see Griffin approaching as the woman he was talking to turns to look right at me, disappointment washing over her expression.

"Joyce," I answer quickly. "I need to talk to Joyce."

"About?" he questions with a raise of his eyebrow.

I deflect. "Is she here? Can you find her for me?"

The phone on the desk starts ringing but his gaze never leaves mine. "Why do need to talk to Joyce?"

"Aren't you going to answer that?" I point at the phone.

"No." His eyes drop to the front of my T-shirt. "My partner's assistant will pick it up."

As if on cue the phone stops mid-ring. I turn my attention back to him. "I came here to see Joyce."

"She has the day off." He shoves both of his hands into the front pockets of his pants. "It looks like you'll need to settle for me."

Chapter 8

Piper

I open my black leather wallet and slide out forty dollars. I look down at it. "Joyce loaned me this the day I was robbed. I've been meaning to stop by to repay her, but it kept slipping my mind."

Griffin leans closer, his voice lowering, his breath skirting over my cheek. "I've already reimbursed Joyce. Keep it."

I won't knowingly be indebted to anyone. I hold out the bills in front of me. "Take it."

His hands stay hidden within the pockets of his perfectly tailored pants. "No, Piper. I insist on you keeping it. You're already out the money that bastard took from you. Consider this an offering to make up for that."

I clutch the two twenty dollar bills in my fist. "I don't expect you to replace what he took from me. You had nothing to do with what happened that night."

He finally tugs his hands free before he crosses his arms over his broad chest. "The son of a bitch was carrying around my business card."

"How does that matter?" I question with a tilt of my head. "You're not responsible for what he did. Joyce loaned me this money so I want to give it back to her."

It takes a beat but he extends his hand, his large palm outstretched.

I push the bills into it but he's too quick. He closes his hand over mine. I stare up into his face, my eyes searching his for any sign that he feels the same sudden spark inside that I do.

"Let's compromise, Piper," he says quietly. "This isn't enough for a good dinner, but it will cover a drink. Meet me tonight at the bar around the corner. We'll call it even after that."

I try to jerk my hand free but his grip is too tight. He wants more than a drink. I see it in his eyes and feel it in his touch. He's looking at me with the same lust that he did that first day I stood in this office.

The only thing he knows about me is that I wear short dresses when I'm out partying and I slept with a stranger. That's not who I am. My one-night stand was a one-time deal. I won't go down that road again and I sense that one fuck is all that Griffin is looking for.

"I appreciate the offer." I give my hand a hard yank and he lets it drop. "We're even now. I paid back what I owed."

"I'd like to buy you a drink."

I know that lawyers are notorious for being persistent, so I don't take it as a compliment that he's still pressing for more. "I'm not interested."

A cocky smile slides over his full lips. "You're interested."

"I'm busy." I tuck my wallet back into the brown leather bag slung over my shoulder. "I have a lot of work to do. Please thank Joyce for me. She really helped me out."

"Work?" He arches a brow in response. "Joyce mentioned that you're an artist."

The details I gave Joyce were sparse. I told her I got a job at the Grant Gallery and that I was an artist. I didn't expand on that because the stilted grin on her face at the time, told me that she didn't care. I can always tell if art strikes a chord in a person when I first mention that I create it.

I nod. "I am."

"I'm not, but I appreciate genuine talent when I see it."

I scan the walls of the reception area and the generic framed prints that are hung there. "Do you think the artwork in here reflects genuine talent?"

"I think the art in my apartment does."

A smile tugs at the corners of my mouth. "I take it no one has ever accused you of being subtle? Are you inviting me back to your place to see your paintings?"

"That's not what I meant, but if you're offering to come to my place…"

"I'll pass," I interrupt with no hesitation. He's obviously hot-as-hell, but he's also a distraction that I don't currently need. "Thanks for loaning me your assistant when I got into trouble. Have a good day, Mr. Kent."

"Griffin," he corrects me. "Good luck with everything, Piper."

I'll need it. I'm three days away from teaching my first art class in New York City. The next two months will make or break my career. I can't let anything screw this up, not even a sexy-as-sin lawyer in an expensive suit.

***

"Are you planning on sitting in for my first class?" I ask Bridget as she adjusts the frame on one of her portraits that she just hung up.

She's sold two today. I admit I envy her. I can't imagine the rush in knowing that someone is willing to pay a small fortune to own a piece of your work.

I've sold some of my drawings in the past, but those were at art fairs in Denver where no one was willing to pay more than twenty dollars for an unframed sketch.

"I wish I could." She brushes a piece of lint from the frame in front of her. "I promised my boys I'd be at their soccer practice tonight."

She told me this morning that she has two sons. I waited while she scrolled through the picture library on her phone to find just the right image to show me. They're gorgeous and judging by the big smiles on their faces in the photograph, they're also very happy.

"You need to be at that practice," I stress the point. "My class will go off without a hitch."

She turns her attention to the sleeveless black dress I'm wearing. She skims her hand over the belt before she adjusts the collar. "You look sophisticated. Your students are going to be impressed from the moment they walk into the studio."

I know I have more than an hour before class starts but my nerves are already in high gear. I spent most of the weekend preparing the studio, the supplies and the lights. I have everything set to go, including a brief introductory speech about myself. I also want to touch on what I hope my students will get out of the class.

"I'm going to run up to the studio and double check that I have all bases covered." I smooth my hair over my shoulders. "Wish me luck."

"You don't need luck, Piper. You have something better than luck. Talent. You're going to blow your students away tonight. Mark my words."

Chapter 9

Griffin

The last thing you want to see when you walk into a room is the woman you're interested in talking to a naked guy.

That's the sight that greeted me when I took my seat in the small studio at Grant Gallery. I was let into the gallery by a security guard who brought me up here. I admit I was late. On a good day I leave my office by nine p.m., so making it here by seven was a stretch. I slid onto the stool behind the empty easel at half-past seven and by then Piper was engaged in a conversation with a guy with a semi-hard dick.

That seems to be finishing up now since she's pointing at a small stage at the front of the studio that she apparently wants him to get up on.

He does. He strikes a pose with his arms over his head, his abs flexed and a side view of his cock.

I'm not coming into this blindly. I read the course outline this afternoon before I hit the registration button. In my imagination, I thought a beautiful woman would be resting on her back on a velvet sofa eating grapes.

I haven't been able to stop thinking about Piper since she showed up at my office on Friday. I don't go out of my way to get any woman into bed, but after researching Piper online, I signed up for her class. I doubt like hell I'll make it past tonight, but that's all the time I need to convince her to have a drink with me. Besides, I wanted to see for myself what she's like when she's leading a group of aspiring artists.

I peek around the easel when Piper starts talking. "Since you all have varying degrees of experience, I thought tonight we'd focus on your vision of what you see before you. I want you to draw Rufus just as you see him. Don't concern yourself with details. This is simply an exercise meant to help me determine how you view the model."

I stare at the blank paper in front of me.

If I had a clue where to start, I might, but instead, I lean over to look at the paper of the woman sitting next to me.

"This isn't Algebra. You can't cheat." She shoots me a look. "I'm Brenda. You're late."

"I'm lost," I admit. "Have you taken one of these classes before?"

She sets her charcoal pencil down. "I'm a first-timer too. Let's say we pair up as study buddies. You can come over to my place after class so we can practice drawing. I'll be your model if you'll be mine."

I'm getting hit on while a naked man is less than twenty feet away. I'll take the ego boost.

"I'll have to pass." I look over to where Piper is standing next to another student. It's a man around my age. I'm tempted to call her over, but I didn't come here to disrupt her work. I came here to learn more about her.

"Suit yourself." She points at my three-piece navy blue suit. "By the way, you have excellent taste in clothing."

I nod in appreciation as I turn back to the easel.

"Pick up the pencil and let the subject speak to you." Piper's voice carries from behind me. "Don't restrict yourself by your own expectations. Let your creativity lead you where it wants to."

It takes a beat before I realize she's talking to me so I respond. "What if my creativity fucked off a long time ago?"

I hear her breath catch. A moment later she steps into the spot next to my stool. "Mr. Kent? Is that you?"

I turn to her and smile. "Hello again, Piper."

Her gaze falls to the blank paper in front of me before she eyes me. "What are you doing here?"

"I'm here to learn. You're here to teach. Let's get started, shall we?"

***

"What's the verdict?" I stand in front of my easel. "Do you think I have a future in charcoal art?"

Piper picks up my sketchpad and holds it in her hands as her gaze takes in every line. "I see promise."

She's polite. My drawing is elementary, at best. I know it. I've never professed to have a talent in the arts. I may hang around for another class or two if it means I can convince her to go out with me.

She places the drawing back before she pivots to face me. "I printed out the list of students who enrolled this morning, your name wasn't on there."

"I'm not crashing." I clear my throat. "I signed up late this afternoon."

"Why?" She flinches as she looks back at my easel before her gaze settles on my face. "Joyce told me that you aren't a fan of art."

"How exactly did that come up in conversation with my assistant? "I ask in a low tone. "Were you asking her about me?"

Her cheeks blush with the question. "No. I mean…yes…we were talking about a lot of things. Art happened to be one of them."

"Have a drink with me tonight and fill me in on what else you and Joyce talked about."

"I can't."

"You can't?" I step a little closer.

She half-shrugs but doesn't offer anything beyond that.

"Another night then?" I rub my jaw; irritated that this isn't going the way I want it to. "Consider it a thank you for teaching me how to draw."

Her perfectly arched brows rise. "I haven't taught you anything yet."

I'd love to push her to break her plans so we can have a drink followed by a night in my bed, but she just went through hell two weeks ago. I need to slow the pace and give her time. "You're going to teach me to draw like you, aren't you?"

"Like me?" Her hand flies to the middle of her chest and my gaze follows. There's enough cleavage to suggest a perfect pair of round tits. The dress she was wearing in my office the day we met showed off a curvy ass. My teacher is hot-as-hell.

"Perhaps not exactly like you." I take a step back. "I hope to see some improvement in my skills by the end of the course."

She looks toward the studio entrance when Rufus, the now-clothed male model, walks in. "I'll see to it that you improve. That's my job."

"Are you ready, Piper?" he calls from where he's standing.

"Class is dismissed." She smiles. "I need to lock up, so I'll follow you out."

An unwelcome knot of jealousy forms in the pit of my stomach as I brush past Rufus and try to block out the sound of Piper laughing at something he's saying.

I signed up for eight weeks of this shit. I'm beginning to wonder why the fuck I did that.

Chapter 10

Piper

"I think our first class went well, Piper, what do you think?"

I nod as I walk toward my apartment with Rufus by my side. "I think so too. The range of talent in the class is vast."

"I hear you." He taps on the shell of his ear. "That guy in the suit should ask for a refund. Unless you're a miracle worker, he's wasting his time and money."

"Hey," I playfully hit him on the arm. "I get paid a commission for each student. I need every single one of them to tough it out until the end."

He smiles down at me. "I guess I do too. What's an art class without students?"

"Late rent," I joke. "That's my building up ahead. You're sure you didn't go out of your way walking me home?"

"I live four blocks west." He jerks his thumb to the right. "We can ride the subway and walk together after every class. I get that you probably feel unsafe after that jerk stole your wallet."

When Rufus stopped by the gallery last week to drop off his contract, he overheard me telling Bridget that I'd picked up a new phone. She mentioned the robbery and Rufus jumped into the middle of our conversation with his sage words of advice.

He showed off a few defensive moves that he told me I could use in the future if I run across the thief again. After that, he offered to walk me home after class so I wouldn't run into any more trouble.

I accepted because I knew that I'd enjoy the company.

"I'm trying to put it in my past," I admit as I dig in my purse for my keys. "It was one bad experience. I don't want it to ruin my time in New York."

"Are you here temporarily or long-term?" He stops at the steps to my building.

"I'm not sure yet." I shrug. "I feel like this is the place for me to be if I want a career in art, but the competition is fierce."

"You're one of the most talented artists I've worked with." He takes a seat on one of the concrete steps. "I've been around the block a few times in the industry and when I checked out your stuff, I was blown away."

I settle down next to him, not sure if he's being genuine or not, but the compliments are hitting a sweet spot inside of me. "Are you serious?"

"Dead serious." He evens his tone. "You need to pursue this, Piper. Put everything you have into it. You're going places."

He's not an expert on charcoal art, but he does offer some unique insight that I wouldn't find anywhere else. "I'll give myself six months since that's how long I leased my apartment for. "

He stands. "Six months is good. I've been here a little more than a year and my career is finally starting to take off. We're not shooting for the same stars, but I know the struggle to get noticed."

That's hard to believe, given the fact that he's so good-looking.

I follow and slide to my feet too. "Thanks for the company on the walk and the advice."

"That's what friends are for." He adjusts his backpack on his shoulder. "I've got an early call time tomorrow for a shoot. I'm going to take off."

I watch him walk away. He's a nice guy, but there's no spark there. I can't say the same for Griffin Kent. I almost forgot to breathe when I first saw him in my class. He may be the kind of man I don't need right now, but he's definitely a man I could want.

***

I use the watering can I found in the office to give each of the plants in the gallery a drink. I came in this morning to talk to Bridget about my first class. She'd sent me a text message late last night asking about it.

I was already fast asleep, so as soon as I woke, I typed out a message to her telling her I'd stop by the gallery once it opened to fill her in. She's becoming a friend and it's a relationship I want to nurture since my only friend to speak of at the moment is Rufus.

We shared a coffee once I got here and I told her how the class went off without a hitch. She was impressed and promised that she'd sit in on one next week.

"Piper?" she calls from where she's standing at the back of the gallery. "I need your opinion on something."

I finish watering the last of the plants before I walk to where she is. "What's up?"

She gestures to an empty spot on the wall that holds her portraits. "I have to replace the one that was bought this morning. I have two to choose from. I need your expert eye to help me decide."

I'm humbled. I nod. "I'd be honored to help with that."

She reaches down to pick up a black square frame. She holds the back toward me so I can't see the portrait until she flips it over near the wall. "I love this one."

My eyes skim over the frame and the sketch inside. My breath stalls. "Bridget, that's mine."

She smiles as she places that one down before picking up the second frame. "I like this one too."

I shake off the disbelief that she's framed two of my pieces. I had left my sketchbook in her office the other day when I was working in the studio. She promised that she'd lock the door so no one would wander in and take it. "I don't know what to say."

"Say you're happy that we'll be selling your work in the gallery and say you'll consider taking on a second job with me during the day."

I scratch my chin. "You want me to work here during the day?"

"The woman I hired to help manage the gallery when we first opened, retired a couple of months ago and I'm not cut out for full-time." She glances at her watch. "I love taking the boys to school in the morning, but I miss being there when they're done. I'm looking for someone to take over afternoons here. You'd be responsible for sales and helping me with promotional materials. There's some light cleaning. It's all easy and I pay well."

The burden of looking for a second job is instantly lifted from my shoulders. "I'll take the job."

"Can you start after lunch?"

I look down at the red pants and white blouse I'm wearing. "If I meet the dress code, I'll stay for the day."

"You look stunning as always, Piper." She reaches back down to grab the first framed nude drawing she showed me before she hangs it on the wall next to her portraits. "Let's hope that you sell your first piece on your very first day."

Chapter 11

Griffin

"You're skipping out on pool tonight because you have an art class?" My friend, Sebastian Wolf, follows the question with a hearty laugh. "Your bullshit excuses for bailing on me are getting worse and worse."

"Do you hear me bitching when you cancel on me?" I draw a pull from the beer in my hand. "How many times have you sent me a text saying you can't make it?"

"I work homicide," he points out. "A dead body trumps a pool game any day of the week."

"In that case, a hot art teacher trumps a pool game."

That catches his full attention. He puts the phone in his hand down on the top of the weathered bar we're sitting next to. He asked me to meet him at Easton Pub after he was done his shift. I agreed even though it was only five o'clock and I had a meeting scheduled.

I don't see him as often as I'd like because his work dictates his life. I can say the same for myself. That's why I had Joyce reschedule with my client so I could jump on the subway and head here.

He twirls the glass of bourbon in front of him. "You're taking an art class because the teacher is hot?"

"Essentially, yes." I agree as I take another sip of beer.

He lowers his head to hide the smile on his lips. "You know I need to ask, Griffin. Since when do you put in that much time and effort to score?"

It's a good question. I don't have an answer to it.

"She ended up at my office a couple of weeks ago." I start at the beginning because I'm hoping that will help him piece this together. "She was robbed after a one-night stand. The guy dropped my business card on the floor and she came looking for me."

"Who was the guy?"

I shrug as I take another drink. "I haven't figured that out yet."

"So she shows up and what? You decide to take her class because you feel sorry for her?" He chuckles. "Where the fuck is the real Griffin Kent because he wouldn't do shit like that?"

He's right. I wouldn't. I'm not known for my giving nature.

"I like this woman," I admit with a shake of my head. "Don't ask me why, but I do."

"Apparently, you like her enough to sit through an art class. What kind of class is it?"

I could lie. I should lie, but I don't bullshit Sebastian. We've been friends too long for that. "It's a nude drawing class."

He throws his head back in hearty laughter. "You're shitting me. You're taking a class where you draw nudes?"

I try not to smile, but it's useless. "What the fuck is so funny? You don't think I can do it? Is that it?"

"What does the model look like?" His dark brows wiggle. "Is she as hot as the teacher?"

"He's average." I push back the bite of jealousy that I still feel whenever I think about Piper with Rufus. "He's got nothing on me."

"He's got enough confidence to show his dick to a room full of strangers." He lifts his glass to his lips. "I'll give the guy credit for that."

I'm not about to give Rufus credit for anything. He's just a hurdle on my path to Piper. She's as attracted to me as I am to her. It's only a matter of time until we act on it.

***

"I'm thirty-two." I don't look over at Brenda because I've been trying to avoid engaging in her one-sided conversation for the past hour. I've been successful up to this point.

"You're thirty-two?" She raises her voice loud enough that everyone around us turns to look, including Piper.

I keep my pencil on the paper even though it's not moving. "Why is that so hard to believe?"

"It's not that it's hard to believe." I catch the motion of Brenda's hand in my peripheral vision.

The woman is on top of her game today. Our assignment was to focus on an outline of Rufus. Her drawing has clean lines and a discernable shape. Mine doesn't.

"I would have pegged you for right around my age." She taps the tip of her pencil on the sleeve of my suit jacket. "I'm twenty-eight."

That warrants a complete turn on my stool to face her. "You're twenty-eight?"

"And a half." She throws me a smug grin. "Don't look so surprised."

"You're misreading disbelief for surprise." I brush my hand over the charcoal dust she left on my sleeve. "You're not twenty-eight."

That draws her brows up. "You're not a gentleman if you question a lady's age."

"How are you two doing?" Piper approaches from behind Brenda. "I'm glad to see you talking. Sometimes it can help if you bounce ideas off another artist. There's also the benefit of moral support, of course."

"I think mine is perfect." Brenda sets her pencil down on her easel. "What do you think, Piper?"

Piper steps up until she's standing between Brenda and me. The side of her white pencil skirt brushes against my pant leg as her fingers moves in the air close to the sketchpad sitting on Brenda's easel. "I'm impressed. I think this is a great foundation to work from. It's important to keep scale in mind. You don't want his thigh to appear smaller than other areas."

His dick. She's referring to his dick.

Brenda's interpretation is off the mark. The cock in her drawing is scaled up. It's at least two times larger than the thigh she just drew.

I look up at Rufus. He's still in the same pose he was an hour ago.

"You're doing great, Griffin." Piper's hand lands on my shoulder. "I'd pay more attention to cleaning up the lines."

I would too if I gave two shits about the sketch I'm creating.

"I'll keep that in mind." I reach to cover her hand with mine when I glance up at her face.

Our eyes lock as she lets out a small sigh. "I need to check on the other students."

She doesn't move until she hears someone call out her name and with that, she tugs her hand free and finally walks away.

Chapter 12

Piper

"So what's going on between you and the suit?" Rufus asks casually as we sit at a table on the patio of his favorite burger place after class.

"The suit?" I place my purse on my lap for safekeeping. Since I was lucky enough to get almost everything back after that horrible night, I've been diligent about where my belongings are at all times. I even lock my purse in the desk in the gallery's office ever since Bridget gave me a set of keys. I know that the door to the office is locked too, but I like the added assurance.

Rufus looks over the paper menu with a quick glance. "You had your hand on his shoulder. There were little pink hearts in your eyes. I saw it all from where I was standing."

"You're talking about Griffin?" I prop my elbows on the table. "Nothing is going on between the two of us."

"You should tell that to the chemistry sparking between you two that every person in our class could sense." He points at the menu. "I'm going to order us both cheeseburgers. You're not a vegan, are you?"

I give my head a shake. I usually don't eat dinner this late at night, but I'm starving. "I love burgers too much. Do they come with fries?"

"The best fries in the city." He looks over at the sidewalk and the pedestrians passing us by before he gazes across the table at me again. "You need to watch out for guys like Griffin."

I cock my head to the side. "Why?"

"They run through women like water." His hand moves to cup the empty water glass in front of him. "I've had too many female friends hurt by guys just like him. They're always one and done."

"One and done?" I repeat back with a laugh. "As in, one night together and then it's done?"

"You know it."

I'm not bothered by what he's saying. I've suspected that Griffin isn't looking for anything but a casual hook-up since we met. How can I fault him for that when I jumped into bed with a complete stranger less than a month ago? "I try not to judge anyone before I know them. Griffin asked his assistant to help me when I was in a bind. I don't think he can be all that bad."

"Don't let those little pink hearts in your eyes blind you." He studies me. "Keep your guard up at all times. You don't want a man to get in the way of your career."

I know Rufus means well, but his words irritate me. I don't need him to be a protector, just a friend. "I can take care of myself. I'm not as naïve as you think. I am hungry though. Can we order?"

Rufus considers what I said before he raises his hand in the air to signal a server. "I have no doubt you're more than capable of taking care of yourself, but if you need a shoulder to lean on, I've got two."

***

I scan the wall of portraits in the gallery before I look over at Bridget. "Did you change out my other drawing for this one?"

She doesn't look up from the screen of the open laptop in front of her. "No."

I study the sketch again. I thought she hung the sketch of a woman I drew when I was in art school, but now it's a piece I completed a few months ago of a man. I turn back to look at her. "Are you sure? I could have sworn that you hung up the sketch of the woman."

"I did." She finally glances in my direction. "I sold that this morning so I replaced it with your other drawing."

I stand in stunned silence. This is a moment I'm never going to forget. I've waited my entire life for this and now that it's here I don't know how to react.

"You should be proud of yourself." Bridget walks to where I am. "It sold as soon as we opened. In fact, the man who bought it was waiting outside the door before I unlocked it. He's been in before."

I look down to where my hands are shaking by my sides. I grip the skirt of my red dress to quiet them, but it does little good. "I'm surprised it sold so fast. I expected it to be sitting there for months."

"He walked right over to it." She touches the corner of one of her framed portraits to straighten it. "The last time he was in the gallery he was looking for you."

"For me?" My stomach flips. The only man who would hunt me down at this place is my dad and since he has an extreme fear of flying, I know it can't be him.

"Yes. I told him to check out the website for your classes. He might be one of your students. He's about six-foot-two with brown hair and blue eyes. He's super handsome."

Griffin Kent.

"I don't officially start my shift for another hour. I'm going to run an errand." I walk toward the office where I left my purse. "You're good with that, right?"

"Take your time," she calls after me. "You should go out for a celebratory drink. It's not every day an artist sells their first piece so fast."

Chapter 13

Piper

The offices of Kent & Colt are much different than the two times I've been here before. It's not because they painted the walls or rearranged the furniture. Joyce isn't behind the reception desk and the chair isn't vacant either. The woman who is sitting there has light brown hair, she looks to be my age, and her view of relationships is blatantly obvious.

"So you think that it was love?" she asks into the phone against her ear. "Love is so fucking overrated. If you are naïve enough to believe a man when he says he cares about you, the heartache is on you. You and only you are responsible for that shit. Do you hear me?"

I stand and listen because there's no other option at this point.

"Lawrence is the biggest asshole you'll ever meet." She glances at me before she casts her gaze back down to her blood red fingernails. "The only reason you're with him is because of his net worth. Don't even try to deny it."

I clear my throat because I need to be back at work soon and her conversation doesn't seem to be nearing an end.

She holds the phone close to her chest and looks up at me. "What can I do for you?"

"I'm here to see ..."

"You and half the women in this city," she interrupts. "Let me guess…you had the most incredible night of your life with him and you're worried that he lost your number since you haven't heard from him since."

"No, it's not like that at all." I scurry past her words, not wanting to engage in any conversation that includes details of Griffin's sex life. "I'm just wondering if he's available."

She drops her phone on the desk and mimes air quotes. "He doesn't do relationships so, yes, he's available."

I'm tempted to turn and walk out. I don't see how it makes good business sense to have this woman meet and greet the public, but I shoulder on. "Can you call him and see if he'll come out here to talk to me?"

"Dylan's busy," she begins with a heavy sigh. "You'll have to sit and…"

"Piper?" Joyce pops her head out of one of the many offices. "I thought that was your voice."

I turn to where she's exiting the office and coming toward me. I wouldn't have considered her a friendly face until now but compared to the woman I've been talking to, Joyce is a saint.

"What are you doing here?" She stops short of where I am. "Did you find out who the man was who robbed you?"

The woman behind the desk finally ends her call. "Joyce, man the phones. I'm going to lunch."

Joyce rolls her eyes as the woman steps away from the desk. I can tell there's no love lost between the two of them.

"That's Fiona." Joyce walks over to the reception desk. "Ignore her. She's pissed at the boss and was unloading to a friend on the phone. I'll have a talk with her later."

I wave my hand in the air as I nervously chuckle. "It's fine. I think she thought I was here to see Griffin's partner."

Her brows pop up. "Dylan Colt is his name. He had a brief fling with Fiona before Griffin hired her on. She keeps trying to pick up where they left off. Dylan keeps everything between them strictly professional. Today she's on a crusade to warn all of her friends to avoid men."

I'm instantly grateful that I don't have to deal with workplace drama. "I'd like to see Griffin if he has time."

She looks at the screen of the computer sitting on the desk. "His next appointment isn't for another thirty minutes. I'll walk you back to his office. He'll be glad to see you."

"Are you sure you shouldn't call him to tell him I'm here?" I point at the phone in her hand, unsure of how Griffin is going to react when I show up in his office without warning.

"I know Mr. Kent better than he knows himself. " She steps toward me. "Follow me, Piper. I promise you my boss will have a smile on his face the moment he sees you."

***

"If you're anyone other than Joyce, you're fired. If you're Joyce, you should have knocked."

I look past Joyce's shoulder to where Griffin is standing near a window. His back is to us and he has one hand pressed against the glass. He's wearing a pair of black pants and a white button-down shirt. The sleeves are rolled up to his elbows.

"I don't knock when I bring welcome visitors." Joyce takes a measured step into his large office. It's decorated in masculine tones with a large glass and steel desk as the focal point. "Piper Ellis is here to see you, sir."

He turns to face us. "You can go, Joyce. Shut the door and hold my next appointment until Ms. Ellis leaves."

I'm tempted to reach over and grab Joyce's arm to stop her in place. Her short blonde curls bounce as she nods. "If you need anything, sir, you know where to find me."

I stand silently as I hear the door click shut behind her.

Griffin rests both of his hands on the edge of his desk and leans forward. He looks like an animal studying its potential prey. His tongue darts out to wet his full bottom lip before he finally speaks to me. "To what do I owe this pleasure?"

Chapter 14

Griffin

I know exactly why Piper Ellis is standing in my office in a gorgeous red dress. Her boss shared the good news.

I spotted Piper's drawing on display when I walked through the gallery on my way up to the studio for class last night. It caught my immediate attention because on that massive wall of framed sketches, it was the only one that showcased the nude body of a woman.

I went back this morning to buy it. It's an intriguing piece.

Her gaze darts around my office, before it lands on the drawing in question. It's now hung above a brown leather couch in a seating area I reserve for client meetings. I had the maintenance staff take care of it immediately after I arrived here from the gallery.

"You bought my sketch," she says quickly as she looks back at me.

"You're welcome, Piper."

She holds her clutch purse close to her stomach. "Why did you buy it?"

I don't move from where I'm standing even though I want to stalk toward her. I don't trust that I won't reach out to touch her. "I view it as a solid investment."

That lures her two steps closer to me. "How so?"

"You're obviously talented." I stand up straight shoving my hands into the front pockets of my pants. "The value of that piece will only increase, no?"

She looks at the framed sketch again. "It will. I'm still surprised that a man like you has any interest in art at all."

If it's an insult, she's delivered it with a small smile. I push for clarification because the cat and mouse game we're playing is making me hard. "A man like me? Expand on that."

She closes the remaining distance to my desk with several sure steps. "Your office is devoid of any emotion, except for my sketch which you only bought today. Typically, people who appreciate art do so because they see something in it that others don't."

"I see a beautiful woman." I nod toward the sketch.

She glances at it before her gaze falls to the floor. "I see more."

I round my desk at a leisurely pace until I'm standing behind her. She doesn't move to turn. I lean forward so my breath whispers over her long slender neck. I want to pull the pins from her hair and watch the brown waves tumble around her shoulders, but I bite back the urge. "Tell me what you see."

She looks to the side. It gives me a perfect view of her profile. Small nose, soft angled brow and a set of perfectly plump lips that would feel like heaven wrapped around my dick.

"I see vulnerability."

So do I when I look at her.

"What else?" I question as I inch closer to her back.

Her eyes dart to mine before she skims the sketch again. "Pain. Look at her face. You see that she's been hurt."

I close my eyes briefly. I know all too well what pain looks like. I see it every morning when I look in the mirror.

"She wants to love herself but she can't." She slicks her tongue over her bottom lip. "She's trying to hide her imperfections. That's why she has her arms draped over her stomach."

I take another look at the drawing. The woman in it is stunning. Most people who took a quick glance at the sketch would consider her body perfect. "Did she tell you all of this when you drew her?"

That turns her on her heel until she's facing me. She looks up. "No. I felt it when I drew her. I see it now when I look at the sketch."

"What do you see when you look at me?"

She tries to step back, but the desk stops her. She drops her clutch on it before she grips the edge with her hands. "What do you mean? I see a lawyer."

I move forward, pinning both my hands next to hers. She doesn't flinch when I lean close and whisper, "You see more than that."

"Anger. Disappointment. Pain."

My eyes squeeze shut. "Everyone feels those things."

Her breath sweeps over my lips as my eyes open and lock on her hers. "At others. You feel it within. It's directed at yourself."

I suck in a heavy breath. She's either insightful beyond her years or a mind reader.

"You're not denying, counselor." She looks at my lips.

I inch forward almost brushing my mouth against hers. I need to change the fucking subject before more of my soul is bared to this woman. "Has anyone ever drawn you nude, Piper?"

Her left brow pops up in surprise. "That's none of your business."

"Answer the question." My shoulders tighten.

She sucks in a breath. "Yes."

"Who?"

Her eyes lock on mine before she looks toward the floor. "One of my professors."

She's not as difficult to read as I thought. The dilated pupils, the slight increase in breathing, the break in our gaze. They're all indicative of guilt. I've seen it enough times in my work. A cheating husband, an unfaithful wife, a Swiss bank account funded by a business one spouse didn't realize existed. "You slept with him."

Her lips part and a breathy gasp escapes. "I'm not talking about this."

My cock swells even more with the mental image of her being fucked from behind in a studio much like the one she teaches in now. "Was it before or after he drew you?"

Her hands leap from the desk and land on my chest. She doesn't push back. She's not anxious to escape the cage I've trapped her in. "You can't ask me that."

"I can and I have." I lean even closer until I can taste her breath when she exhales. "It was before, wasn't it? He fucked you and then he took to his easel and captured his conquest."

"It wasn't like that," she protests with a weak bump of her fist to the middle of my chest. "I wasn't his conquest."

"What was it like, Piper?" My grip on the desk tightens as I fight back the urge to claim her mouth with mine. "Tell me what it was like."

Her voice is unsteady as her gaze falls to my lips. "He was my conquest. I'm the one who seduced him."

Chapter 15

Piper

It's a confession I've never made to anyone. I haven't told a soul that I slept with Professor Mitchell during my senior year of college. He was in his mid-thirties at the time, sexy and the most talented man I'd ever met.

"You seduced him?" Griffin's voice is thick and raw.

He's aroused. I felt it when I turned around to face him. He's hard beneath the fabric of his pants. The desire to kiss me, to take me, is there in his eyes. He hasn't touched me though.

I nod. I'm not ashamed of what I did. I wanted Haywood Mitchell from the first moment I saw him. The draw toward him was intense and as each week passed in his class, my courage grew.

It wasn't until we were alone in his studio one night after his students' mid-semester show that I made my move. I kissed him. He didn't resist and within the hour, he was inside of me.

"How many times?" His gaze searches my face. "How many times did he have you?"

My pulse thrums in my neck at the jagged, rough timbre in his voice.

"A few," I say quietly. "It only happened a few times and then it was over."

The intimate part of our relationship was short-lived. Haywood was seeking tenure and his trust in me was limited. He convinced himself that I'd tell everyone on campus about our hook-ups and his chance at the job of his dreams would evaporate into thin air.

Griffin steps even closer until his body is pressed against mine. I can feel every hard plane of his chest and abdomen through his dress shirt. His erection is tempting me. The urge to grind against him is there, but I can't. I won't.

"Who ended it?" he grits out, his jaw clenched. "He'd be a fucking fool to walk away from this."

This.

His gaze says what his mouth doesn't as he looks me over. My nipples are tight and furled beneath my dress. There's an ache between my legs and even though he can't feel it, he has to know. My breathing gives it all away. I'm on the cusp of panting.

"It ran its course." My eyes drop to his chest. "We had fun, but it ran its course."

"You're lying," he accuses as his hand flies to my chin. "He ended it. It hurt you, didn't it?"

"It doesn't matter." I shake my head to rid myself of his heated touch, but it's useless. He only applies more gentle pressure as he nudges my chin up until our eyes meet.

"I'm a lawyer, Piper. I know when someone is lying."

"Why does it even matter to you?" My chest tightens. I drop my voice to a low whisper. "You don't know me and it was forever ago. I'm sure as hell not interested in your past relationships."

"Your lip twitches when you lie."

I bite the corner of my bottom lip to stop its quiver. "I'm not lying. This is ridiculous. I came here to ask you why you bought my sketch, not so you could interrogate me about one of my ex-lovers. My past is none of your business."

"You want me to know." He smiles like he believes wholly in his own words.

He's right to have that smug look on his face. I do want him to know. I want him to know everything about me, but I sure as hell won't give him the satisfaction of telling him that.

"I didn't come here for this." I arch my neck back to try to gain at least a few inches of separation between his lips and mine. "I want you to let me go."

"Let her go, Griffin," a deep voice from behind him startles us both. "Jesus Christ, man. What the hell is going on here?"

When I twist my neck to look past Griffin's shoulder, he finally slides his hand from my chin.

A handsome black-haired man in a gray suit is standing in the doorway. He's taller than Griffin, his shoulders broader. His eyes are a vibrant light blue.

As he approaches, I feel Griffin tense against me.

"This doesn't concern you, Dylan."

"Like hell, it doesn't." He's next to Griffin now, his hand resting firmly on his shoulder. I watch him as his gaze sprints over my face before he speaks to me. "I'm Dylan Colt."

"Piper Ellis," I say without thinking.

"Piper Ellis," he repeats back as he looks at Griffin's profile.

"She's not a client." Griffin turns his attention to Dylan. "Piper is my art teacher."

A smile teases Dylan's mouth. "Your art teacher?"

"I teach a class at Grant Gallery." I push against Griffin's chest and this time he acquiesces. He steps back allowing me the space I need to move to the side. "Griffin is one of my students."

"You're her student?" It's obvious that my words surprise Dylan. "What exactly did I interrupt just now? A disagreement over your grade?"

His grin is infectious, but it only draws a scowl to Griffin's face. "It's none of your business. You should have knocked."

"You have an emergency hearing with Judge Whittaker in thirty minutes." He taps the face of his large silver wristwatch. "I worked magic to make that happen so get your ass down to his chambers now."

Griffin turns to me. "I have to cut this short, but we're meeting for a drink after class tomorrow."

I glance at the floor before I answer. "I have plans with Rufus."

He rounds the desk to grab his suit jacket from the back of his chair. "Cancel your plans with him. You and I are having a drink tomorrow night."

He's wrong. We're not.

Whatever happened just now between Griffin and I can't happen again. I need to keep my eye on my career. A man as intense as Griffin Kent can derail my future and I'm not about to take that chance.

Chapter 16

Griffin

"So now you're an artist?" Dylan picks up a bottle of imported beer. "When exactly did you decide to take an art class?"

I may be closer to Dylan than I am to my brother, but I'm not about to tell him that I enrolled in Piper's class because I want a taste of her. He'll use that information against me for the next ten years. "I'm trying to broaden my horizons."

"Don't bullshit me, Griffin." He takes a healthy swig. "Did Draven put you up to this?"

My older brother has more influence over me than I'll readily admit, but I haven't heard from him in weeks. That's expected. Draven runs his own home construction business. He pushes himself physically until he's bone weary, day after day after day. "Draven has nothing to do with this. It's not a big deal. You play basketball a couple of nights a week. I take an art class. What's the difference?"

"No one I play basketball with looks like Piper Ellis." He squints at me. "Did you sign up for that class because of her?"

I want him to drop the subject so we can move on to the reason we met at this restaurant in the first place. Work. It's what we talk about ninety-nine percent of the time. "She's interesting."

"She's gorgeous." He laughs. "Did you try and pick her up and she turned you down? Is that why you're chasing after her like a stalker?"

"She came to see me today." I point out with a tilt of my bottle in the air. "I'm not stalking her."

"You looked about ready to fuck her against your desk." He raises his bottle and taps it against mine. "Cheers to my untimely arrival in your office."

Piper wasn't even close to kissing me when Dylan barged into my office earlier. Her resistance was melting, but she was holding back. I have no idea if that's related to whatever the hell is going on between her and Rufus, or not. "That wouldn't have happened. She's been hanging out with the model from class. Rufus is the guy's name."

"Rufus," he echoes. "What kind of class are you taking?"

I look down at the table. If I don't tell him, he'll be on his phone in a minute flat looking up Piper's name. He'll find the class, and the non-stop ribbing will commence. I can't win this. "Human figure drawing. We draw nudes with charcoal."

He freezes in place with the bottle of beer resting against his bottom lip. "Repeat that."

"You're an asshole." I finish my beer. "You heard me."

He puts his bottle on the table. "Let me get this straight. You signed up for an art class in order to fuck a woman, but now you're drawing her boyfriend's dick?"

"Jesus." I shake my head as I laugh. "It sounds fucked up when you put it that way."

"It is fucked up." He leans back when the server places our meals on the table. "I'm not going to tell you how to live your life, Griffin, but old wounds can take years to heal. Don't fuck yourself over just to get a woman into bed."

I don't need the reminder of my past. "Thanks for the advice, but I'm good. I came here for a breakdown of the Johnson case. If you're serious about me taking it over, I need to get up to speed."

Dylan can read between the lines. He knows I'm telling him to back the hell off. He picks up his fork and knife. "Understood. Let's eat and then it's all business."

***

"What's that thing on his nose?" Brenda points at the paper in front of me. "Is that a wart? Did you draw a wart on his nose?"

I was going to draw it on the side of his dick, but I'm not a jealous teenager with a warped sense of humor. I'm a professional who has no problem controlling his temper in a court of law, yet I can't push back the irritation I feel every time I glance at Rufus to see his eyes pinned to Piper's body.

The white pants she's wearing make her ass look like a ripe peach. The blue top she has on is clinging to her tits. Every guy in this class has to be rocking a hard-on tonight.

Rufus sure as fuck is. I'm guilty of it too.

To that end, I adjust my pants and move my ass on the hard wooden stool. Brenda's gaze drops to my lap.

"I'm free after class." Her hand lands on my thigh. "I'm eager to please if you know what I mean."

I look over at her as I grab her hand to lift it off my leg. Her lips curve into a wide-mouthed '*O*' before her tongue trails over them. She's offering to blow me. Again, I take it as a compliment since she's been staring at Rufus's dick all night. "I'm busy, Brenda."

"I'm not against a threesome." She looks at my lap again. "I swing both ways so I'll do whoever you're doing."

"I swing one way," I clarify. "I like women."

She gestures toward Rufus. "I thought you were into him considering you've been hard since class started."

"His dick does nothing for me." I go back to looking at my drawing. It's crap. I know it. Piper knows it. She made a point of not mentioning my sketch when she cruised past Brenda and me ten minutes ago. She tossed a compliment to Brenda but didn't say a word to me.

"It does something for me," she says quietly. "I get off after every class thinking about Rufus."

For fuck's sake. I need to get the hell out of here.

"That's it for tonight." Piper moves to stand at the front of the studio. "I hope you'll take some time this coming weekend to visit the Sem Jansen exhibit at Origin Hall in SoHo. It opens on Saturday afternoon. His focus is the nude male form. I find his work inspiring. We can discuss it next week."

I'd rather cut off my left big toe than spend another second staring at more dicks.

"I take it you're not going to that?" Brenda closes her sketchpad before turning to face me. "I was going to suggest we check it out and then head back to my place."

"Thanks, but no." I stand. "You're on your own."

"Do you think Rufus would go with me?" She watches as he wraps a white towel around his waist. "I'm obviously not your type. Maybe I'm his."

"It doesn't hurt to ask." I should warn her that Rufus is hooking up with Piper, but she'll figure that out on her own soon enough.

I watch as she rounds her easel and marches toward Rufus. Brenda's cute, but she's no match for our teacher. I glance at Piper as she speaks to two female students. Her gaze volleys between their faces and the scene playing out five feet away from her.

As subtle as she thinks she is, there's no mistaking that she's interested in what's going on between Rufus and Brenda. Maybe I misjudged what she feels for the model. If she didn't give a shit about him, she wouldn't keep glancing his way while he charms a giggle out of Brenda.

The muscles in my jaw tick as I approach Piper when the two women standing next to her take off in the direction of the studio door.

"He only has eyes for you," I whisper into her ear from behind.

Turning, she faces me, her shoulders squaring. "They're talking about the exhibit in SoHo. Brenda wants to tag along with Rufus and me when we go on Saturday afternoon."

Brenda wants to a lot more than to be the third wheel on their mid-day date. "Sounds like a treat."

"It wouldn't hurt you to go, Griffin." Her lips thin as she lets out a breathy sigh. "You could use some inspiration."

I clear my throat, pushing back the urge to tell her that I want her to come home with me. *No, I fucking need her to come home with me.*

The shape of her lips, the emerald green of her eyes and the sweet scent of her skin is all the inspiration I need to fuck her senseless which was my goal when I signed up for this class. "Inspiration is everywhere. I'm heading out to find some now."

I step away as Rufus and Brenda walk toward us. The cocky grin on Rufus's face says it all. He knows I want Piper. He may have won this round, but I'm just getting started.

Chapter 17

Piper

"I ordered too much pizza. Do you like pepperoni with extra cheese?"

I look to my left and the now familiar sound of my neighbor's voice. Jo and I have bumped into each other a few times in the shared corridor since I moved in. We never exchange more than a couple of words about the weather, but every time, I'm always greeted by a bright smile on her face.

This time is no different. She's sporting a wide grin. She's dressed in navy sweatpants and a grey sweater. Without the dark makeup that usually circles her eyes, she looks younger.

I passed on Rufus's invitation to stop for pizza on the way home from class. I was hungry but not in the mood for his company. Pizza with Jo sounds much better to me tonight.

"I'd love some." I turn my key in the lock of my apartment door. "Your place or mine? I've got a bottle of red wine we can share."

"My place works." She motions beyond the door she's propped open with her foot. "Do you want to change first? I'd hate for you to spill tomato sauce on that get-up."

I laugh. I'm wearing white slacks and a blue short sleeve sweater. In my world that's a magnet for stains. "I'll put on something else and then head over."

"Come straight in. I'll get the plates ready." She glances back at me before she disappears into her apartment.

She may be old enough to be my mother, but there's no age limit on friendship.

I duck into my dark apartment, race to my bedroom, and change my clothes.

***

"You're from Denver?" Jo swipes a paper napkin over her lips as we sit cross-legged on an area rug in her living room next to the coffee table. "So you've seen the mountains?"

My dark blue Denver University sweatshirt gave me away. I pulled that on along with a pair of cut off denim shorts and flip-flops before I grabbed the only bottle of wine I have and made my way to Jo's apartment.

I expected it to be a mirror image of mine, but it's not. Jo's place is larger. The walls are painted a warm gray. Her furniture is nicer than mine too, but that's to be expected. I rented my plain white-walled, one bedroom furnished.

"You can see them from my parents' place." I take another bite of the thick-crusted pepperoni pizza. It's better than any pizza I ever had back home.

Jo swallows a mouthful of the cheap red wine that she poured into two glasses while I served up the pizza. "I've never seen mountains in person. Why would you leave a place like that to come here?"

I didn't hesitate when Bridget offered me the job with her studio because I've always wanted to live in New York. I can't say it's exactly how I pictured it would be in my mind's eye, but I've only been here a few weeks.

"Don't get me wrong," Jo goes on as she lifts another slice of pizza from the cardboard box. "I love New York, but it's almost impossible to find peace here. I'd give anything to have a week in the mountains. I'd finally be able to hear my thoughts."

"It is a lot quieter there," I say quickly. It's going to take some time for me to get accustomed to the blaring car horns and the non-stop sounds of Manhattan. "I was offered a job at a gallery here, so I took a chance that I'd fall in love with this place."

"Oh, you will." She laughs. "This city has a way of burrowing into the deepest parts of your heart and holding tight. I'd never leave but I sure as hell could use a break every now and again."

I chew on another bite of pizza as she studies my face.

"Are you an artist?"

I nod. "I do charcoal drawings. I'm teaching a class at a gallery uptown."

"You're chock full of surprises." Her entire face brightens as she takes another sip of the wine. "You must be really good if you're teaching."

The corners of my lips tick up in a small smile. I'm proud of my talent. I've been honing it for years. "There's always room for improvement, but I'm good. I think I'm really good."

"You have more confidence than the last girl who lived in your apartment. If I'm being honest, you have more confidence than the last three tenants combined."

I tuck my hair behind my ears before I ask the obvious question. "Have you lived in this building for a long time?"

"Longer than I care to admit." She winks. "It's my home now, so I'm staying put."

I've never focused too far in the future but in an abstract way, I've always pictured myself getting married and having kids someday. I'm tempted to ask Jo if she's a mom but that feels like way too personal a question at this point.

"Every girl before you has left because she fell in love while living next door." She jerks her thumb at the shared wall between our apartments. "One told me I was her good luck charm so keep that in mind when you cross paths with a looker."

I've already crossed paths with the best-looking man I've ever seen. I turned Griffin down again tonight. As I watched him stalk out of the studio, I had an unexpected burst of regret. A man like that would have no trouble finding someone to hook up with him.

I'd bet my last dollar that right now, he's naked in someone's bed.

Chapter 18

Griffin

"What the fuck, Griffin?" Dylan rounds the corner into his kitchen wearing only a pair of black boxer briefs. "I didn't give you the key to my apartment so you could waltz in here whenever you damn well please."

"Let me guess." I reach for a glass tumbler from the cupboard above the sink before I pour myself two fingers of the best scotch I could find at the liquor store down the street. "Light brown hair, blue eyes, the body of a dancer."

"Fuck you." Dylan rakes both hands through his black hair. "I was mid-thrust when you started yelling that you were here. You scared the shit out of both of us."

"What's this one's name?"

I let that hang in the air between us. It's a dick move. We have an unspoken rule. I don't bring up the bullshit from Dylan's past and he leaves mine buried. Tonight, my callousness is fueled by the two drinks I had earlier.

"Go to hell," he spits back.

"You don't know her name, do you?" I slide the bottle across the marble counter toward him. "You don't know because you don't give a shit."

He picks up the bottle and downs a swallow. "What do you want, Griffin? Why are you here?"

I scrub my hand over the back of my neck. I don't have an answer to that question. I left Piper's studio with the intent of going to the office to go over my notes before court tomorrow morning. The Lindel case is on the docket and I have every intention of squeezing every cent I can out of Lana's client.

I didn't make it to my office. I stopped by Easton Pub after spotting Sebastian inside with his new partner, a rookie detective. After introductions, I bought them both a beer while I nursed two glasses of scotch. By the time I left, they were heading out too. Sebastian offered to share a cab with me, but I told him I had work to do.

I ended up here after trying to call Dylan about a case file while I was waiting for the subway. He didn't pick up and even though it was near midnight, I made my way to his apartment for no other reason than to drag him into the pit of misery I'm drowning in.

"It's that fucking art class, isn't it?" He takes another drink from the bottle. "Why the hell did you think it was a good idea to enroll in that? You had to know it was self-torture."

How many years have to pass before the debilitating pain of loss finally leaves every cell of your body? I know for certain it's not one, or five. What's the magic number? Ten? Twenty? Fifty?

"Piper's class has nothing to do with the past." I grip the edge of the counter tightly with my left hand. "Don't bring it up, Dylan. Don't."

"Don't?" he echoes back in a low voice. "You're the one who walked in here and ruined my night. You don't get to dictate what we talk about."

"I ruined your fuck," I correct him with a sly smile. "So you didn't get to shoot your load in a woman who looks like Eden tonight. Boo-fucking-hoo."

He's on me in an instant. His fists bunched around the lapels of my suit jacket. "Shut your mouth. Don't say her name to me."

"Who's Eden?"

The sound of a breathy feminine voice turns both our heads in the direction of the hallway. I know what she'll look like before I see her. Tousled sun-kissed locks of light brown hair, big blue eyes and lean legs. The only thing she's wearing is a dress shirt. It's blue, pinstriped and a match to the one Dylan was wearing when I left him at the office earlier to go to Piper's class.

"No one," Dylan lies through his teeth. "Go back to bed, beautiful."

"Who are you?" Her gaze skims my face. "Are you staying?"

Fucking a woman that Dylan's had his dick in isn't going to happen. We've never touched the same pussy and that's not about to change.

"He's no one too." Dylan loosens his grip on my jacket. "He was just leaving."

I should send her out the door and confront my best friend about his reckless need to relive his past with every woman he fucks. I'm not a therapist though and my demons can rival his any day of the week.

"I'm out." I pat Dylan on the cheek as his one-night stand retreats to his bedroom. "Get back to it, buddy."

"Fuck you," he whispers. "Sober up, Griffin. You're due in court at nine a.m. and I'm not covering for you this time."

He won't need to. I have a French press at home and a pound of my favorite beans. I'll spend the next few hours with hot coffee in hand while I drink my way back to reality.

"Tell what's-her-name I'm sorry for the interruption."

He looks up at the ceiling before he takes a step back. "Go home and get some sleep and for fuck's sake, quit that art class."

I should, but I won't. I can't get Piper Ellis out of my mind and no amount of scotch, coffee, or sleep will change that.

***

"We should celebrate." Lana stands next to me as we watch both our clients exit the courtroom. "That went much smoother than I anticipated."

Her high-pitched voice only adds another layer of intensity to the rhythmic pounding that's been going on inside my head since I woke up this morning. I haven't been this hung-over in years.

"We can start with a late breakfast and see where that leads." Her hand lands on my shoulder. "That scruff of beard on your face makes you look extra wild, Griffin. I'd love to feel that on the inside of my thighs."

The whiskers covering my jaw are a testament to my inability to lift a razor this morning. I barely managed to shower and dress before heading over here.

I take pride in the fact that I visit the gym before the crack of dawn four mornings a week. I carve out time for a healthy breakfast and I shave every day, but today the scotch still had its claws in me when I woke up. I'm not even sure my boxer briefs made it on under my black suit pants.

"I can't fuck you," I answer without looking at her. She resembles a sexy librarian today with her hair pulled back into a stylish bun, black eyeglasses perched on her nose and a tight navy blue suit hugging her curves.

Lana could be the remedy for what ails me. A celebratory fuck with her might chase Piper out of my mind, but it would be temporary. I fell asleep last night with my cock in my palm after blowing my load all over my stomach while I was thinking about my art teacher.

I'm fucked.

"Why not?" Lana moves to step in front of me so I have no choice but to face her. "The case is over. There's no conflict of interest anymore. We can go straight to my place, get into bed and we'll both be back in our respective offices by two o'clock."

"I drank too much last night."

She smiles and reaches to adjust my tie. "I thought you looked a little green around the edges. I know the perfect cure for that."

"Don't say it's your pussy, Lana. It can't heal me."

"I beg to differ, but I was going to say the fried egg tacos at this place I go to in midtown."

I swallow hard. "That sounds fucking disgusting. I'm nauseous. The last thing I need is food right now."

She grabs hold of my forearm. "Trust me, Griffin. This is my go-to when I hit a bottle of red wine too hard. An hour from now you'll be thanking me."

I don't argue with her. We still have a few details to finalize on the Lindel case. This will give me a chance to close the file on that and make it clear to Lana that we're never fucking each other again.

Chapter 19

Piper

I scan the inside of the diner until I spot a familiar face. I head toward the counter and the one empty stool next to it.

"I thought you were the one who slid this free breakfast coupon under my door this morning," I say to Jo as she places a white ceramic mug filled with coffee in front of me. "Is this thing even real?"

I wave the pink sticky note attached to a white envelope at her.

I spotted it as soon as I walked out of my bedroom less than an hour ago. It was impossible not to see it on the floor near my apartment door.

My first name was scribbled across the sticky and inside the envelope was a small rectangular piece of paper. There were only two things handwritten on it with blue ink, an address to this diner and *Free Breakfast Before Noon.*

I showered before I dressed in jeans, a light green sweater and black ankle boots. When I left my apartment, I knocked on Jo's door. I wasn't surprised that she didn't answer since I saw a stack of pink sticky notes on her coffee table last night.

"If the owner of this dive says it's real, it's real." She reaches for a silver carafe. "This is cream. It's the real stuff. Do you want one splash or two?"

"One." I inch to the left to grab a single packet of white sugar from a small bowl. "Will you thank the owner for me?"

"You just thanked her yourself."

My head whips up. "What? You own this place?"

"Crispy Biscuit is all mine." She slides a paper napkin with the diner's name printed on it toward me. "If you're ever looking for me and I'm not at home, I'll be here."

I take a minute to soak in the décor of the small eatery. There are at least a dozen tables, some crowded with people sitting on wooden chairs. Several booths line the wall of windows that overlooks the sidewalk. They're all occupied too.

There are no unnecessary, over-the-top design choices. The walls are painted white. The floor is covered by a checkerboard pattern of black and white tiles. It's a quintessential New York City diner.

"I already love this place." I turn back to Jo. "What do you recommend for breakfast?"

A redheaded woman dressed in jeans and a black T-shirt with *Crispy Biscuit* written in pink lettering across her chest approaches from the left. She tucks a small pad of paper and a pen in the white half-apron tied around her waist. "I need an order of three scrambled egg whites with no salt or pepper and a half slice of grain bread, not toasted and no butter. Fire up a hangover special to go with that."

"A bland scramble with grain bread?" Jo peers into the packed diner. "I only know one person who orders that. Where's my Lana?"

I turn to look in the direction of Jo's gaze. I immediately spot a woman with her arm in the air waving enthusiastically. She's pretty, blonde and smiling broadly. That has to be Lana. Just as I'm about to turn back to ask Jo who she is, another hand darts into the air next to Lana's.

I squint, sure that my eyes are playing tricks on me. They're not. A grinning Griffin Kent is staring at me from across the diner and I can't look away.

***

I glance down at the bagel that Jo plopped in front of me before she took off to talk to Lana. She didn't offer any explanation about who the woman is, but judging by the tight embrace they shared when she practically ran over to Lana and Griffin's table, I'd say they're close.

As tempted as I was to take the toasted bagel and side of cream cheese to go, I didn't. Jo told me to stay put because she wants me to try the special of the day. I told her the bagel was more than enough but the frown on her face said it all.

"Of all the greasy spoons in this city, I walk into yours."

I smile inwardly when I hear Griffin's voice next to me. I haven't glanced over at his table since he broke our stare when he reached into his pocket to pull out his phone so he could answer it.

I clear my throat as I turn to look up at him.

Jesus. Griffin Kent with a light beard and ruffled hair is going to be the star of every fantasy I have for a very long time.

He must have rolled out of bed with Lana to share breakfast for two at this place.

"It's not mine," I answer quietly. "My next door neighbor owns this place. She knows your… your friend."

"My friend?" His face is unreadable. "You're talking about Lana?"

I've never outright hated a name before, but if I never hear the name *Lana* again, I won't complain. She's the one he went to after I turned him down last night. I did this to myself so it makes perfect sense that karma brought me to this diner so I could come face-to-face with my regret.

I nod. "Do you two come here often?"

"Do you always blush when you're jealous?"

I scrub my hand over my cheeks. I never blush. At least I don't think I do. "I'm not blushing and I'm not jealous."

"You're both." He leans his elbow on the counter. "How are your weekend plans with Rufus and Brenda coming together? Are you three still hitting up that art exhibit on Saturday?"

"Why?" I bite back with a sugary sweet grin. "Do you and Lana want to join us?"

His eyebrows rise. "The five of us on one date? As fun as that sounds, I'm not free on Saturday. I'm heading out of town for the day."

"Work?" I ask as I steal a glance behind him at Jo and Lana before I turn my attention back to his face.

He stares at me for a beat, looking into my eyes. "No. It's a personal trip."

Even though I sense that he wants me to ask for more details, I don't. We barely know each other, and besides, he's on a breakfast date with someone else. "I'll be discussing the exhibit in class on Monday night, so you'll hear all about it then."

"I can't wait." He leans in to lower his voice. "It's always a pleasure seeing you, Piper. Always a pleasure."

The last word hangs in the air between us as he walks back to his table and the woman I have no right to envy, but I do.

Chapter 20

Piper

Jo swipes a towel over the top of the counter chasing away the crumbs left behind by my bagel. "Your breakfast special is coming right up, Piper. You should count your lucky stars that Jerry is back from his break."

"Who's Jerry?" I ask with a tilt of my head.

"The cook," she says as she refills my coffee. "He's been with me since day one, but lately he spends more time taking breaks than he does behind the stove. I have to fill in and it's not my favorite place to be."

"When was day one? How long have you owned this place?"

"Coming up on fifteen years now." She purses her lips. "I started as a waitress. When the owner was ready to sell, I jumped at the chance."

I don't see how I can segue this conversation into one about Lana, so I stay on topic. "That's a big leap. You're a brave woman."

"I didn't move across the country to a city where I didn't know a soul." She chuckles. "That takes courage, Piper. You've got it in spades."

I dump the contents of another packet of sugar in my coffee mug before swirling it around with a small silver spoon. "I've never considered myself brave."

"You're fearless."

I decide to test her theory by asking the one question that's been dancing on the tip of my tongue since Griffin and Lana left the diner five minutes ago. I didn't glance over at them as they ate and when they got up to leave, I tapped out a text message to my dad. I couldn't risk looking at Griffin only to find him holding hands with Lana.

"From where I was standing, it looked like you and Lana's friend get along well," Jo says before I have a chance to ask how she knows Griffin's breakfast date.

Since I still don't know her connection to Lana, I answer simply and truthfully. "Griffin is one of my students."

Her brows go up. "He's in your art class? Good for him. I wish Lana would take time for herself like that."

I jump at the opportunity to finally broach the topic of the woman Griffin spent the night with last night. "I could see how much you and Lana care about each other. She seemed really happy to see you too."

"She's a good girl." A smile teases the corners of her lips. "She first started coming here when she was living on campus. I'd feed her breakfast every morning in exchange for dishwashing on Saturdays. She told me today it helped her get through law school."

"Lana's a lawyer?"

"Just like your student. They came here from court." She looks back toward the kitchen. "She ordered him the breakfast tacos. It's a cure-all for a hangover."

"They drank too much last night?" I ask before I give any thought to it. It doesn't matter if they both got falling down drunk. It's not my business. I shouldn't even be having this discussion with Jo.

"He drank too much," she corrects me with a sly smile. "I jumped to the same conclusion, but Lana told me she noticed he looked off when she saw him in court this morning, so she was doing him a friendly favor by buying him breakfast."

A friendly favor? They were in court together, not in bed together.

"I'm going to check on your food, Piper. When I get back, I want to hear more about the mountains."

I nod. I felt a glimmer of relief, but it's gone now. Griffin may not have slept with Lana last night, but that doesn't mean he spent the night alone.

I swallow another mouthful of coffee, wishing the hot liquid would chase away this growing need I feel inside me to know everything there is to know about Griffin Kent.

***

"A messenger delivered something for you earlier, Piper." Bridget points at the office when I walk through the door of the gallery.

I had just enough time after eating breakfast at Jo's diner to go home to change for work. I slipped into a pair of dark slacks and a light blue blouse. My wardrobe, outside of jeans and T-shirts or sweatshirts, is limited. I make a mental note to stop at the vintage shop I pass when I walk here from the subway stop. I should be able to find a few decent pieces that won't cost too much.

I set down the two cups of iced coffee that I picked up on my way here. I've had more than my share of coffee today but I plan on sorting through my sketchbooks tonight, so I need the jolt of caffeine to get me from here to there.

"How was class last night?" Bridget calls after me as I make my way to the office to lock my purse in her desk and to retrieve whatever the messenger brought for me.

I slide my purse into the bottom drawer before I relock the desk and tuck the key back into the front pocket of my pants. "It was good," I call back to her as I scan the office looking for anything that remotely resembles a delivery.

"It's that envelope in the middle of my desk." Bridget appears in the doorway. "It was hand delivered by a man in a black suit."

I pick up the cream-colored envelope and run my fingertip over the dark ink that spells out my name. There's no return address.

"Did he say who sent it?"

"No, but we can find out if you rip it open." She laughs as she takes a step forward. "I've been itching to find out what it is since he dropped it off."

I look up to where she's now standing. "When was it dropped off?"

She bounces in her red sandals. "Thirty minutes ago. I'm dying of curiosity. A mysterious man brought you an envelope. Open it, Piper."

I nod as I carefully run my fingernail under the flap. My heart is hammering in my chest. This envelope is nothing like the one Jo slid under my apartment door. This one is luxurious. Its quality is evident. I reach in to pull out a thick card.

"What does it say?" Bridget inches up on her heels. "If it's not too personal, that is. If it is, I'll understand."

My gaze falls to the plain card that is embossed with the faint outline of a rose. I flip it open and read the words to myself.

You have been selected to attend a private showing of Sem Jansen's collection tomorrow evening. 8.p.m.
Origin Hall. Manhattan, New York.
No cameras allowed. No additional guests, please.

My hands are shaking as I hand the card to Bridget and watch her expression transform from curiosity to shock.

"Piper," she practically screams my name into my ear when she tugs me into a hug. "You know Sem Jansen? I've been a fan of his forever. Oh my God. I'd give anything to go to that private showing."

I take the card when she offers it back. I reread every word, absorbing each syllable. "I wish you could come with me."

I sincerely wish that and it's not just because I can tell that it would mean the world to her to meet one of the most respected artists in charcoal drawings.

I want her there with me because I don't know what's going on.

I don't know Sem Jansen. There's no way in hell he knows who I am. He's from Amsterdam. The last time he set foot on North American soil I was ten-years-old.

She cranes her neck to look at the invitation again. "They always keep the guest list to a minimum for these things. It's usually art critics, collectors, those types."

"Why was I invited to this?" I mutter to myself before I look at her. "I was planning on going to his exhibit on Saturday with Rufus and one of my students."

"Sem must know your work, Piper." Bridget's hands dart to my shoulders. "Beck mentioned meeting him once years ago. Maybe Sem follows our website and he saw your portfolio and he was blown away like we all are by it."

I shake my head. "If he were looking at the website, this invitation would be for you, not me."

"It doesn't matter why you were invited." She starts back toward the gallery. "You're going and I want every last detail when I see you next week."

I nod in agreement even though my mind is racing in a thousand different directions. Tomorrow night I'll be at a private early showing for a legend. Life doesn't get much better than this.

Chapter 21

Griffin

I sort through the files on my desk searching for Morgan Tresoni's. Even though I finished every bite of the breakfast taco platter Lana ordered for me earlier, I still feel queasy. I could get Joyce to run to the Roasting Point Café two blocks over to get me another coffee, but I decide to head out to fetch it myself.

I pay her too much to have her run errands for me. Besides, I could use the fresh air.

"I hear that you killed it in court today." Dylan appears in the open doorway of my office just as I'm about to stand. "You got Mrs. Lindel everything she wanted. Good job."

"Everything but a future with her family intact." I shake my head. "She's torn up about the end of her marriage. The money will make her life easier, but it's not a cure-all."

"It never is." He takes a seat in one of the two black leather guest chairs in front of my desk. "She'll survive. Her kids will pull her through."

He's right. She will. Candy Lindel is a fighter. She'll turn her focus from her bastard of an ex-husband to her kids. That will be her solace as she heals over the next few months.

"I'm going to grab a coffee. Do you want one?"

He shakes his head. "I want to talk about last night."

"Who you fuck is your business, Dylan."

He clears his throat. It's a subject we never talk about. Dylan confessed his past sins over a pint of beer one night in college. That was ten years ago. Since then, I'm the only one who brings it up. I only ever do it when I feel the walls of my own past closing in on me.

It's a defense mechanism. I know it. Dylan does too, but it's still an asshole move on my part.

"Don't go there," he bites out. "I'm trying to take into consideration how shit-faced you were when you showed up at my place."

He's trying to let it go. He's a bigger man than I'll ever be.

"I had a few drinks with Sebastian." I shrug it off. "The scotch got the better of me."

He rubs his jaw, his eyes surveying my face. "It had nothing to do with your art teacher?"

It had everything to do with her, but I'm not about to own that. "I got drunk. It happens. There doesn't have to be some deep, dark reason for me to indulge in too much scotch."

"I've known you for a decade, Griffin." His gaze narrows as he stands. "I know all the deep, dark reasons for everything you do."

He does. Unlike Dylan, I've brought my past mistakes into not only our friendship but also our practice. He's always there to clean up after me even if it means he bears more than his fair share of the workload.

"Thanks for the reminder," I say sarcastically with a grin. "The one you were with last night was cute. Are you going to see her again?"

I already know the answer to that question. She's not Eden, a girl he met in high school. She took off with a piece of his heart after the worst night of his life.

He'll be caught in his never-ending quest to find a woman who can measure up to her for the rest of his life.

"You know that I won't." He looks down at my desk. "I have no complaints, Griffin. I live my life the way I want. You need to start doing the same."

If I thought that was possible, I would, but when you carry the weight of someone else's dreams on your shoulders, it leaves little room for your own.

***

When I walk into the Grant Gallery, I'm surprised to see Piper standing alone, dressed very differently than she was when I saw her earlier at the diner.

Her hair is pinned up into a messy pile on the top of her head. She's wearing a black lace top and white pants. I take a beat to soak in the sight of her.

Jesus, she's a beautiful woman.

When she looks up from the sculpture in her hands, her eyes catch mine and I swear to fuck I see the same spark in them that I feel every time I look at her.

"Griffin?" She places the sculpture down carefully. "What are you doing here?"

I could ask her the same. I didn't expect her to be here in the middle of the afternoon.

"It's my assistant's birthday tomorrow." I smile in an attempt to put us both at ease. I don't want the woman to think I'm stalking around Manhattan hot on her trail. This is the second time today that we've run into each other unexpectedly. "I didn't realize you'd be here."

"I work here now." Her gaze slides from me to the door. I can't tell if she's hoping someone else walks in or not. "I'm here every afternoon."

I make a mental note to drop in more often.

"Did you say that it's Joyce's birthday tomorrow?" She runs her long fingers over a stray strand of her hair.

I watch every move she makes, captivated by how sexy she is, even though it's obvious she's not aware of it. I snap myself out of the trance with a shake of my head. "She's in love with the sketch that I bought; your sketch. I came to buy one for her."

A small smile settles over her face. "You're going to give Joyce one of my sketches for her birthday?"

"Show me what you've got." I close the distance between us with several steps.

Her head tilts as she studies me. "I'll show you the pieces that Bridget has framed. You can pick the one you think Joyce will like best."

I stare down at her face. All I want is to kiss her. I want to know what those sweet pink lips taste like and the sounds she'll make when her lips part to let me in.

"I'll go get those sketches." She inches back on her heels. "Don't move. I'll be right back."

I nod. I'm sure as hell not going anywhere. There's no place in the world I'd rather be right now than in this gallery.

Chapter 22

Piper

If I knew that I'd run into Griffin again today, I would have taken an extra five minutes to do something with my hair. I stand out of his view in the office as I attempt to tuck the uncooperative strands back into place atop my head. It's useless.

I skim my hands over my cheeks to chase away the heated feeling that rushed through me as soon as I turned and saw him.

He looks just as irresistible as he did this morning. The only difference is that he's lost his tie, unbuttoned the top two buttons of his dress shirt and the shadow of stubble that was on his jaw earlier is gone.

My lungs expand on a deep breath as I pick up the four frames that are sitting on a table in the office. Bridget showed them to me yesterday before I went to the studio for my class. She had helped herself to my sketchpad again and the results were stunning.

Each of the frames contains a sketch that I'd long forgotten about. Two of them are of the same woman. The others are of a man I drew years ago. His back was to me as I sketched every sharp detail of his body.

They all have unique traits that make me adore them and even though I feel a bittersweet twist around my heart at the thought of selling them, I know that it's a step forward in my career.

"I have these four and there's one on the portrait wall," I say as I walk back into the gallery cradling the frames in my arms.

Griffin's head pops up. His fingers stall on his phone's screen when he sees me standing a few feet away from him. "Let me help."

"I'll put them here." I motion toward a rectangular table with my elbow. Bridget uses it when she's cataloging new inventory. It's also the perfect place for her to sit while she talks about art over a cup of coffee or tea with a potential buyer. I haven't done that yet since the only thing I've sold is one sculpture and that was to the mother of the artist.

I place the frames down carefully, adjusting them until they line up.

Griffin's gaze sweeps over my face before he studies each sketch. His index finger trails over the bottom of the frames. "I have no idea which one to get."

I try to contain my smile. I point at one of the drawings of the woman. "If Joyce liked the sketch you have in your office, I think she'd be happy to have this one."

He crosses his arms over his chest. "She'd be happy to have any of them. Last year on her birthday I got her a ferry ride out to Ellis Island to see the Statue of Liberty and a box of cupcakes."

I catch his eye. "I'm sure she appreciated it."

"She didn't." He laughs through his response. "The ferry ride was free and the cupcakes were dropped off at the office earlier that day by a client as a thank you to me for a job well done."

I shake my head and bite back my own laughter. "So you're trying to make up for last year by buying her something she actually wants for her birthday this year?"

"You could say that." He turns to face me. "I'll take the one you suggested although I'm tempted to buy them all."

I look up at him. Bridget priced each sketch at more than I ever would have. The cost of all four together is twice my monthly rent. "That would be one hell of a birthday present."

His arm brushes against mine as his hand dives into the inner pocket of his suit jacket to tug out his wallet. "I'm only giving one to Joyce. I have someone else in mind for the others."

Who? I want to blurt out, but he didn't offer, so I won't go fishing for details.

I take the credit card. "I'm sure they'll appreciate the gift."

Goosebumps crawl up my skin when his hand touches mine. We linger like that, our fingertips pressed against each other, his card dangling between my index finger and thumb.

"I'll be sure to tell them all about the artist."

"You don't know much about me." I finally slip my hand away from his although the heat of his touch lingers on my skin. "What will you tell them?"

His eyes close as he sucks in a deep breath. When he finally opens them, he narrows his gaze. "I'll say that you're an incredibly talented, beautiful woman."

He thinks I'm beautiful.

"I'll say that I'm fortunate to be in your class even though I'll never master the finer points of figure drawing."

"There's always hope," I whisper. "I see promise when I look at your work."

"You're lying." His gaze drops to my mouth. "Your lip is quivering."

Before I can bite it, the pad of his thumb is on it. He slides it along my bottom lip, slowly, so painfully slowly that I almost moan.

"I'm not taking your class to become the next Sem Jansen."

I smile against his thumb. "Why are you taking it?"

"You know why." His breath whispers across my lips.

I lean closer wanting him to kiss me. His hand drops when my lips part and just as my eyelids flutter shut, the bell above the gallery door rings.

I close my eyes wishing that whoever walked in just now would turn around and walk out.

"I take it you're Piper?" An unfamiliar male voice asks.

I look briefly at Griffin before my gaze slides to the door and the man standing just inside the gallery.

Oh, shit.

"You're Brighton Beck." I push out the words through a wave of anxiety. "It's good to finally meet you."

***

Black hair, piercing blue eyes and a full sleeve tattoo. All of that is standing in front of me in the form of Brighton Beck, or Beck, as he prefers to be called by his friends, according to Bridget.

I go for the safe approach. "It's nice to meet you, Mr. Beck."

He looks down at the black T-shirt and jeans he's wearing. "I don't seriously look like a Mr. Beck to you, do I?"

How am I supposed to answer that? I haven't exactly made the best first impression. When Brighton walked in, I was just about to kiss Griffin. Brighton's presence pulled us apart and as I finished up the sale for my framed sketches and arranged for them to be delivered to Griffin's office, I didn't glance at either man. They were involved in a discussion about the weather that effortlessly slid into a shared appreciation for the New York Yankees.

Griffin walked out with a smile on his face because Beck invited him to a home game next month.

The man I'm crushing on handled meeting my boss with humor and grace. I wish I could say the same. I silently fumbled with Griffin's credit card before I walked away to ring up his purchase.

"I'm teasing you, Piper." Beck flashes me a brilliant smile. "I want you to call me Beck. I also want you to forgive me for breaking up that moment between you and your boyfriend."

"Griffin isn't...no, he's not...I like him, but," I stammer my way through that before I stop to catch my breath. "Griffin is one of my students. He was here to purchase a gift for his assistant. I'm not his girlfriend."

"My mistake." He walks closer to where I'm standing next to the table that my sketches are sitting on. "This is your work, isn't it?"

I nod exuberantly. "Yes. I drew these. I just sold all of them to Griffin."

"He's got a great eye." He taps one of the frames. "You've got immense talent, Piper. This is impressive. It's good to have you on board."

Chapter 23

Piper

The second I approach Origin Hall I know something isn't right. It's not like I've ever been to a private showing for a celebrated artist before. I haven't.

I've been to my fair share of gallery shows in Denver, but those painters and sculptors were typically friends from school or on a rare occasion, a well-known artist's exhibit would pop up in the city and I'd be one of the first in line to see it.

Tonight, there's no crowd gathered on the sidewalk outside the venue. From where I'm standing, I can't even tell if the lights in Origin Hall are on.

I glance down at the invitation in my hand once more. I've been clinging to it since I left my apartment. I'm wearing my favorite little black dress and four-inch heels, so I decided to come in an Uber.

Jo caught me just as I was exiting my apartment. She was the one who arranged my ride for me since one of the regulars at her diner drives people around Manhattan in his sleek black Mercedes. I've never been in such a luxurious car and even though it cost more than the subway, it was well worth it to avoid the trip here in these heels.

The time printed on the invitation is clear. The event definitely starts at eight o'clock. It's five minutes past now which means I should see at least a few other people approaching the building, but there's no one.

Just as I'm about to reach for the doorknob, the door swings open.

I jump back when I see who is standing on the other side. In my wildest dreams, I thought there might be a slim chance that I'd get to meet Sem Jansen, but I wasn't holding out hope. He's notoriously private and is nowhere to be found at his own exhibits.

He's dressed in white pants and a white button-down shirt. His gray hair is slicked back from his face and his black eyeglasses are perched on the tip of his nose.

"Piper Ellis?" Sem holds out his hand.

I glance down at it, wondering if I'm dreaming all of this. This can't be my life, can it? A few weeks ago I was still in Denver. Now, I'm about to shake the hand of one of my idols.

I reach forward to rest my hand in his. "I'm Piper Ellis. You're Sem Jansen."

His green eyes sparkle when he smiles. "Now that we've established who we are, you should come in. I've been waiting for you."

I don't hesitate when he urges me forward by my hand. I follow him into a darkly lit corridor. I don't hear voices or see anyone.

"Is everyone else already here?" I ask as I look back at the door. "I'm not the last one to arrive, am I?"

"You are the last to arrive." He smiles as he stabs the call button next to an elevator that I didn't notice before. "My exhibit is on the second floor. My other guest is waiting there for us."

One other guest? That's it?

My hands tighten around my clutch purse. It has to be Beck or Bridget. They must have arranged this and didn't tell me. That's the only reasonable explanation for why I was invited.

"Our ride awaits." Sem reaches for the small of my back when the elevator doors open. I step in with butterflies dancing in my stomach and an overwhelming desire to hug the person who set all of this up.

***

I stand frozen in place inside the elevator even though Sem has already stepped off. A part of me wants to hit the button that will take me back to the ground floor.

I know I'm staring. Who wouldn't?

Griffin Kent is standing less than ten feet away from me with a sexy grin on his face and two glasses of champagne in his hands.

He's dressed in a tuxedo, complete with a black bow tie.

"You look incredible tonight, Piper," he says in a throaty tone. "Come and join us."

Us.

Sem Jansen and Griffin Kent.

I have no idea what the hell is going on. Griffin was the last person I expected to see tonight.

He must sense my hesitation because he closes the distance between us with several sure steps. "You can't stand in that elevator all night, Piper."

I look down as if I need confirmation that I haven't moved an inch. I step forward tentatively unsure if my weak knees will support me.

As soon as I exit the elevator the doors slam shut behind me.

Griffin pushes a crystal flute into my hand. I take it and immediately swallow half the glass of sweet liquid. It's delicious. It's also the first taste of champagne I've ever had.

It does nothing to calm me down. I'm sure both men can see my heart thumping in my chest.

"Griffin has shown me your work, Piper." Sem moves to stand next to me. "You have raw talent. With some time and experience, you're going to give me a run for my money."

I down what's left in my glass. I can't tell if I'm freaking out because Sem Jansen just gave me the biggest compliment of my life or if it's because Griffin can't take his eyes off of me.

Chapter 24

Griffin

A million questions are dancing in her eyes and I've yet to answer any of them. I'm following behind her and Sem as they tour his exhibit.

He's taking the time explaining the inspiration behind each of his sketches. Piper's been listening intently, even though she's stolen a few glances back at me.

I haven't been able to read her reaction beyond shock and awe.

The awe obviously reserved for Sem; the shock courtesy of me.

"I didn't know that you'd be here in New York." Piper turns to her side to look at Sem. "I've read online that you don't attend any of your exhibits."

"Don't believe what you read online." He winks at me. "I make it a habit to be on site when my sketches are being prepared for exhibit. I handle the last minute details before I duck for cover and head out of town."

"Does that mean you're leaving before this opens to the public tomorrow?"

"I'll be on a jet headed back to Amsterdam by morning." He sighs. "It's home. It's the place that inspires me the most."

"I still can't believe that I'm standing here talking to you." Piper's gaze darts back to me again before she turns her attention to Sem. "I know you must hear it a thousand times a day, but I'm truly your biggest fan. I love your work. You're the one who inspired me to study art."

Sem moves toward me with a raise of his brow. I know that he's asking for my permission to share something with Piper. I nod because there's nothing he can say to her that I don't want her to know.

"I'm touched by that." He whips back around to look at Piper. "Griffin gifted me with three of your sketches earlier."

A brilliant smile lights up her face. "He didn't? Griffin gave you my sketches?"

Disbelief circles her words as Sem nods. "He knew I'd love them. He was right. I'm going to hang them in my studio back in Amsterdam."

She shakes her head as our eyes lock. "When I mentioned your name in class, Griffin didn't tell me that he knew you."

I bow my head to hide my smile. "That would have ruined your surprise, Piper."

"Griffin helped me out of a bind two years ago." Sem holds up his left hand. "It was a long and very broken marriage."

"I'm sorry," she offers.

"Don't be," Sem counters with a squeeze to her elbow. "I found my inspiration in my ex-husband once and now that we've parted, I've found new inspiration."

She looks over at me. I see something new in her eyes. It's a softness that wasn't there before. "You never know where you'll find inspiration."

I raise my glass of champagne in a silent toast. Her words ring as true for me as they do for her. This woman is inspiring me to want to give her more experiences just like this.

***

"Why did you arrange that for me?" Piper slides onto the backseat of the car that I called for after we said our goodbyes to Sem.

She'd spent more than an hour with him discussing the finer details of many of his sketches. He was open and accommodating as he answered each question she had. His patience was admirable given how exhausted I know he is.

When I handled his divorce, he told me he owed me. We've kept in touch through the occasional email since and when Piper mentioned in class that he had an exhibit in town, I called in the favor.

Her framed sketches weren't part of the deal. I gave those to him as a thank you for taking time to meet with her.

"I could tell that you were a fan." I smile as I settle in next to her. "I knew you'd enjoy the chance to meet the man behind the work."

"Enjoy?" She laughs. "Tonight was the best night of my life."

Is not was. It's not over yet.

"Where are we headed, Piper?" I nod toward the driver. He's silent, waiting for an address.

"I should get home." She nervously plays with the edge of her clutch purse. "I doubt I'll be able to sleep. I just met Sem Jansen."

Those words are music to my ears. She's not ready to call it a night. I'm sure as hell not either. "Let me buy you a drink. I know a place not far from here."

I can see the internal debate in her eyes as she contemplates my invitation.

Say yes, Piper. Fucking say yes.

"I guess one drink would be alright," she whispers before she looks out her window.

It may not be the exact response I was hoping for, but I'll take it. The night is still young and anything can happen.

Chapter 25

Piper

I gingerly sip the martini that I ordered. It tastes nothing like the ones I used to drink in Denver with my college friends. Ironically, it makes me miss them and the simple life I had back there.

When I left my parents' house to move into the dorm my freshman year, I thought my future was in the palm of my hand. Four years and one fine arts degree later, I was back on their doorstep with a pile of student debt and no idea how to earn a living.

They took me in, cleared my financial obligations and sent me out every morning with a cup of coffee in hand and a stack of resumes.

I worked in retail, food service and finally landed a job teaching art in a community center.

When the opportunity to move to New York popped up, my mom and dad were hesitant at first, but they let me go with my small savings account and their blessings.

"Are you thinking about Sem?" Griffin taps his fingers on my hand. "You floated to another dimension there."

I stifle a laugh with another sip of my drink. "I was thinking about home and how dramatically different my life is now."

He takes a swallow of the soda water he ordered. It made me second-guess my choice of beverage, but he insisted I indulge since it was a special night for me.

"What was life at home like?"

I draw in a quick breath. "Easy, quiet."

"Boring?" His brows perk.

I consider that for a second. "No. I wouldn't say that. Life ran at a different pace there. I'd wake up early and work on my unfinished sketches. I'd usually sit on the front porch right after the sun came up."

A ghost of a smile touches his lips. "It sounds very peaceful."

He's incredibly handsome. I've felt a rush of heat flowing over me since we sat down at this secluded table in this quaint bar. He not only looks like heaven dressed in that tuxedo but he smells divine. Add to that the fact that he went out of his way to arrange for me to meet Sem, and I'm ready to crawl into his lap and kiss him.

"Have you always lived in New York?" I ask to break the spell I've put myself under.

"Always," he answers without any hesitation. "It's home to me. I wouldn't say it's home sweet home, but it's where I belong."

That answer is way too intriguing for me to just skate past it without asking more. "Why isn't it home sweet home?"

"New York can be a bitch in her own way." He takes a sip of water and then scowls before pushing the glass away. I can tell he's regretting not ordering something stronger. "The city hasn't always been kind to me."

He's not the first person I've heard talking about Manhattan as if it's a living, breathing being. I suppose in some ways it is. "What has the Big Apple done to you?"

His brows draw together as he studies my face. "It's stolen from me."

"It stole from me too," I joke. "At least one New Yorker did. I think he's a New Yorker."

His shoulders relax with the change of subject. "The police never nabbed that asshole?"

I shrug. "Not yet. I even did a quick sketch of his face and dropped off a copy at the precinct. I thought they could match that to their database and get a hit."

I didn't think it could hurt. The officer at the desk gave me a sympathetic smile when I dropped off the sketch on my way to work one day. I have no idea if he even showed it to another soul. It doesn't matter at this point. I'm over that night.

"You sound like you watch too many detective shows." He leans forward. "My friend Sebastian works homicide with the NYPD. I could get him to take a look at the sketch. Maybe he'll show it around. If the guy who robbed you is a repeat offender, one of Sebastian's buddies might recognize him. "

"If you think it's worth a shot, I can give you a copy of the sketch in class on Monday." I know he's trying to be helpful, but I doubt that anyone who works in homicide would recognize the jerk that took my stuff. He may be lousy in bed, but he didn't strike me as someone capable of murder.

"You can send me a copy tonight." He raps his fingers against my clutch. "Get out your phone so you can program my number into it."

"I'll bring the sketch to class. I don't need your number."

"You want it," he counters, staring into my eyes. "I want yours, so let's exchange now."

I don't move. "I don't want your number."

"The lip, Piper." His hand leaps to my chin. "That adorable way you bite your lip makes me…"

My gaze drops to his lap. I knew I should have taken the seat across from him and not the one next to him. He's too close, and now, he's hard. I can see the outline of his erection through his pants.

"If you're worried I'm going to call you non-stop I can assure you that I won't." He raises his right hand in the air as if he's taking a vow. "I'll keep my distance until you kick Rufus to the curb."

"Rufus?" I hear the surprise in my voice when I say his name.

Griffin rolls his eyes. "The model you like hanging out with."

"I know who Rufus is," I say quickly. "Why did you bring him up?"

He leans so close that I can feel his breath against my cheek. "I don't know what you see in him, but once you get tired of it, I'll be waiting."

I look into his eyes. He thinks I'm dating Rufus. He went to a lot of trouble to arrange for me to meet Sem even though he thinks I'm sleeping with another man. If I didn't fully appreciate the gesture before, I do now. "Why did you set up tonight? Why do all of that for me?"

He brushes his lips against my cheek. It's so soft that it's barely more than a whisper of skin against skin. "You deserve to have every one of your dreams come true."

I inch to the side so his lips are almost touching mine. "Thank you."

"You're welcome." He kisses my cheek one last time before he leans back in his chair "And I won't complain if you throw a compliment my way in class every once in a while."

I laugh. I can't help it. I laugh and even though I know I should tell him that Rufus is only my friend, I don't.

I want the memory of this night to stay exactly at it is. I don't want anything to change what I feel right now.

Chapter 26

Griffin

I eye Piper up trying to telepathically ask her where the hell those compliments are that she promised me on Friday night. Class is almost over and I haven't even received a smile from her.

That's not exactly true. She did offer me a half-grin when I first walked in. I was late, as usual. Today it was almost eight before I slid onto the stool behind my easel. By the time I flipped open my sketchbook and looked to Brenda for advice on our nightly assignment, class was in full swing.

I put the charcoal pencil to paper and managed a few lines around his ankles. I didn't glance in the direction of the front of the class where Rufus is because an ankle's an ankle.

After spending an evening with Piper, I can't stand the sight of the man who will likely go home with her tonight.

"You missed out on a good time on Saturday." Brenda doesn't say my name, but it's obvious she's talking to me. The woman sitting to her left pretended not to speak English mid-way through our first class. I know it's a ruse meant to deter Brenda from talking to her. I just wish I had thought of it first. It's fucking brilliant.

"I had a great time on Friday night," I counter with a killer smile.

Brenda scratches her head. "Blonde or brunette?"

Not that it's any of her business, but I've got nothing to hide. I glance at Piper. I offered to take her home on Friday, but she insisted on grabbing an Uber after we exchanged numbers. I didn't push even though all I wanted was to crawl into her bed. "Brunette. A very beautiful brunette."

"Lucky girl." She tosses me a half-hearted wink. "I had a blast with Rufus on Saturday. Thanks for asking."

I don't give a fuck if she had the time of her life tagging along on Rufus and Piper's date. "Good for you."

"Piper was there too." She motions with her pencil to the center of the room where our teacher is standing dressed in a dark green skirt and white blouse. "She knew a hell of a lot about every sketch. Don't get me wrong. It was interesting and all, but the beers back at my place weren't drinking themselves if you know what I mean."

I take a moment to sketch out a foot complete with five toes. It's not bad. "I take it the three of you took the party to your place?"

"They bailed on me." She sighs heavily as the tip of her pencil glides along the paper before she reaches forward to smudge it with the side of her thumb. "Rufus said he had a friend in town and he wanted to take Piper to meet him. I wasn't invited to that."

I doubt the friend could measure up to Sem Jansen. I've got Rufus beat on that.

"The exhibit goes all week." Brenda rubs her thumb on her jeans transferring the dark charcoal dust. "We can check it out together tomorrow night. I still have a half a case of beer back at my place."

I commend her for her commitment to try and ride my cock, but it's never happening.

"I'm interested in someone else." It's the truth. I haven't been able to look at another woman since I first saw Piper in my office weeks ago. The idea of fucking anyone else isn't on my radar at this point. There's only one woman I want.

"The brunette?" She questions. "I can be a brunette within the hour if that's what you're looking for."

She's a mousy blonde with too much determination. I can't help but laugh at the offer. "As tempting as you are, Brenda, nothing is ever going to happen between us. As I said, I'm interested in just one woman."

"Whoever it is she's lucky." Piper's voice catches both Brenda and me off guard. Brenda turns to face her. I take a beat to erase the goofy grin off my face.

Damn right she's lucky. She'll see it for herself once she realizes Rufus is not the right guy for her. I am.

"I was just about to say the same thing." Brenda whips that pencil in her hand along the arm of my jacket. *Again.*

"Griffin introduced me to Sem Jansen on Friday night." Piper steps closer. "It was incredible."

"You did that for her?" Brenda catches my eye when she glances at my profile.

I nod as I look over my shoulder at Piper. Her hair is down tonight; loose curls are framing her face. She seems content and at ease. "I called in a favor. I'm hoping my final grade will reflect the extra effort."

Piper's green eyes light up. "Your work is improving, Griffin. I don't think you have to worry about your final grade."

I don't give a fuck about my final grade. All I care about is the fact that she's finally looking at me like I'm more than just her student.

***

"Griffin?" Piper calls to me from where she's standing near the front of the studio.

Class ended five minutes ago. I took my time hauling my ass off the stool because I was hoping she'd remember that she has something to give me. I want time together, her body, and whatever else she's willing to share with me, but that's not why I'm hanging around.

"I have a copy of that sketch we talked about." She turns to where she placed her sketchpad. She drops it and her purse on a small table by the stage before every class. I'm assuming that's her routine since I've only witnessed it once.

Class is usually in progress by the time I arrive.

I walk over to her. I was going to mention the sketch as a way to grab a few minutes alone with her. I know she always leaves with Rufus in tow. I want tonight to be different, but if all I get is a few seconds of her time, I'll take it.

Jesus. I'm losing my grip on reality. Since when do I crave a woman's attention?

"I feel funny about you taking this to your friend." She holds the sketch in her hands so all I can see is the back. "You said he works homicide. I don't think the guy who robbed me is the murdering type."

I don't think he is either and I doubt that Sebastian will be any help, but I want to do whatever I can to catch the son of a bitch that fucked her over. She didn't deserve that treatment. Hell, no one does, but the fact that he conned a woman like Piper makes my blood boil.

"Give me the sketch and I'll take it to Sebastian. If he gets a lead, I'll let you know."

"I have a photographic memory when it comes to faces." The paper moves a little in her hands as she tightens her grip on the edges. "This is exactly what he looks like."

I look down when she flips the paper over to show me the sketch.

"I know that asshole." Rage surges through me at the sight of the man's face. "I'm going to fucking kill him."

Chapter 27

Piper

I stare at the screen of Griffin's smartphone. I can't believe my eyes. It's a headshot of a man. He owns an insurance company uptown. He's also the man who took me to bed and then took off with my belongings.

Marco Tresoni.

"How do you know him?" I tear my gaze away from the phone to look at Griffin. He's still angry. It's written all over his expression.

He lowers the phone, cursing under his breath as he looks at the floor. "I'm representing his wife in their divorce."

Divorce? The man I met that night told me that he'd never been married. That was his response when I asked if he had a wife. I wanted the one-night stand but not with a man who made a vow to someone else.

"That's why he had your card," I offer, my mind trying to piece everything together. "He told me his name was Kent. Do you think he was just using it as a fake name or deliberately trying to impersonate you?"

"Either way, he's in deep shit." He rakes his hand through his hair. "I'll rip him apart with my bare hands."

I shouldn't like this side of him, but I do. He's seething mad. I can tell that he's genuinely pissed at this guy for what he did to me. I'm just grateful that now the police can do their job and arrest him.

"I'll go back to the precinct in the morning and tell them I know who robbed me." I feel a sudden rush of relief. I haven't let that night ruin my life but what happened still jars me when I'm alone and I give it too much thought. "I can't believe we figured it out."

That lures a smile to his mouth. "You look happy and I'm ready to toss him in the East River."

I laugh. "You wouldn't really do that."

"Give me five minutes alone with the guy and test me." He fists his left hand. "I can go find him tonight, Piper. I know where the asshole lives."

I step forward to rest my hand over his. He instantly loosens up and cups my hand in his palm.

"We're going to let the police do their job, Griffin."

"Are we?" He moves to rest our hands in the center of his chest.

I stare at them, liking the subtle intimacy, but wanting even more. "I should thank you for solving the mystery."

"We did that together." His thumb rubs circles over my hand. "We should thank each other."

I want that, but he's interested in someone else. I heard him tell Brenda that less than an hour ago. My stance on getting involved, in any romantic capacity, with a man who has a girlfriend or wife hasn't changed. I won't do it, even if I want the man more than I've ever wanted anyone.

I tug my hand free, not wanting to prolong the inevitable.

He exhales harshly when our hands part. "I'm sorry for what happened to you. All you wanted was a one-night stand and you ended up in a hotel room with a sewer rat."

"He's lower than a sewer rat." I shake my head to chase away the memory of Marco's dry, chapped lips on mine. "I should have taken off when he kissed me. It was the worst kiss I've ever had. That was a red flag, but I hung around for more. You know what they say about the way a man kisses."

I catch myself when I realize what I just said.

Griffin isn't one of my girlfriends from back home. I can't talk about sex, good or bad, with him. It's wrong and besides, it makes me want to know how good sex with him would be.

Amazing, mind-numbingly amazing. I know that's how it would be.

"I don't know what they say about the way a man kisses." His mouth curves into a smile. "Tell me."

I laugh nervously as I look down at the floor. He'll see the want in my eyes if I look up at him.

He leaves me no choice when he touches my chin with his index finger. "Look at me, Piper."

I move my head when he applies the slightest bit of pressure to my skin. I look up and into his eyes, knowing that he'll see everything that I've been trying to hide since I first saw him in his office after I'd spent the night with Marco.

"What do *they* say about the way a man kisses?"

I smile inwardly at the way he draws the word '*they*' out. "It's silly. It's probably just a thing women talk about to each other."

"You have to tell me now." His finger runs a path up my jawline until it rests just below my ear. "I can't leave until I know."

I shiver under his touch, hoping he won't leave. I don't want that. If he does leave, I want to go with him. "You can tell things about a man by the way he kisses."

His hand moves to cup my neck. His touch is tender with just the right amount of pressure. "What things?"

The sexual tension is thick between us. I should stop everything and ask him about the woman he was talking about earlier. I want to know who she is and if he's going to be with her tonight. I close my eyes against the assault of an image of Griffin in bed, hovering above someone else.

"Sex," I whisper as I drop my gaze. "If a man is a good kisser, he'll be just as good when he's …"

"Fucking a woman?" He interrupts with a squeeze of his hand on my neck.

I almost moan, not just from the sensation of his touch but the words coming from his mouth.

Fucking a woman. It's raw and visceral.

"Yes," I say under my breath as I trail my gaze over his chest to his face. "That's what a kiss tells a woman."

He licks his lips and I hold my breath for a beat. I want him to show me. I want to feel his lips against mine.

He leans in and every nerve ending in my body fires. I almost lose my balance.

"Tell me you never want to kiss Rufus again." His breath soars over my cheek. "Tell me you're done with him."

I can't let him keep thinking that's what's going on. I need him to know that I haven't kissed Rufus or touched him. "It's not like that with us. We've never kissed."

His brows spike as a sexy grin slides over his mouth. "You've never kissed? I take it that means that you're not fucking him?"

I answer even though my better judgment is nipping at my common sense and telling it to slow the hell down. "Rufus and I are just friends. We're not like you and the woman you were telling Brenda about."

He searches my face with narrowed eyes. "You're jealous again."

"I'm not," I protest, my voice small and unconvincing. I resist the overwhelming urge to bite the corner of my lip when I see his gaze slide there. "I don't care about who you're interested in. It has nothing to do with me."

My eyes shoot to the studio door. I should leave. I should just thank the man for helping me figure out who robbed me, and I should say goodnight and leave my attraction to him behind.

"It has everything to do with you." He leans closer. "You're the woman I was talking about, Piper. You're the only woman I'm interested in."

Chapter 28

Griffin

Rufus has to have a sixth sense when it comes to Piper. He waltzed through the studio door just as I was about to kiss her.

She was open and ready after I told her that she's the only woman I'm interested in. I could tell that my words didn't shock her. Her shoulders relaxed, her lips parted in a soft smile and just as I was about to go in for a kiss, Rufus strolled in and stole the moment and Piper's attention away.

"You ready to head out, Piper?" Rufus walks up behind me wearing torn jeans and a light blue hoodie. "My friend Brett wants to know if we're down for sushi at this place in Hell's Kitchen. He had such a good time hanging out with us on Saturday he wants to do it again."

He looks like a frat boy who hasn't seen a shower in a week. I get that he's got to sell the male model look wherever he goes, but running a comb through his hair wouldn't hurt.

I glance back at Piper. Her gaze volleys from his face to mine. If this is a battle about who is leaving with her, I'm coming out on top.

"I'll take Piper home tonight," I offer without glancing back at him. "We were in the middle of something, Rufus."

"Sorry, dude." He brushes his hand on my shoulder. "I need to talk to Piper too. I'm bummed about a job I didn't get. She's the voice of reason, you know. She lifts me up."

As inspirational as that is, whatever job he didn't get, he'll get over it.

"You didn't get the runway show for Berdine?" Piper brushes past me to stand next to Rufus, her hand resting on his forearm. "I'm sorry. I know you had your heart set on that."

I had my heart set on tasting Piper's lips tonight, but I'm not crying on anyone's shoulders. I'm taking fate into my own two hands.

"Doing that show in London would have changed everything for me." He lowers his head. "My career would have hit the next level. I can't catch a break lately."

Piper glances back at me with a sigh. I can sense what's coming next. She's about to bail on me to comfort Rufus. That's not happening.

"Gabriel Foster owns Berdine." I pivot to face Rufus directly.

"That's not news to me," he drawls through a frown. "I heard he has last say on the models. Guess I'm not his type."

Gabriel's type is petite, blonde and the principal second violinist with the New York Philharmonic. His wife, Isla, hired my brother, Draven, to renovate their main bathroom. When she offered him free tickets to a performance, he handed them off to me.

I spent two hours sitting next to Gabriel while his wife mesmerized him on stage. We talked during intermission and formed an unlikely friendship. The woman I took with me that night wasn't impressed with the concert, but she did land a job working in one of the Liore lingerie boutiques that are under the umbrella of the Foster brand.

Gabriel will do what he can for anyone who asks.

"I'm his type," I quip. "Gabriel's a friend."

"You're shitting me." Rufus pats me on the chest. "Do all you suits know each other?"

"Us suits?" I repeat back.

"You're a nine-to-fiver. You spend your life in an office, right? Gabriel does the same. I figure you all must meet up somewhere after work to blow off steam and kick back with a beer or two."

I don't bother correcting him. My life isn't bound to a time clock. My clients make life-changing decisions day and night. They expect me to be a phone call away. For the most part, I am.

"I'll talk to Gabriel for you," I say it to impress Piper but it's not going to cause me an ounce of pain if Rufus is clear across the Atlantic.

Piper may not see him as anything other than a friend, but his eyes are glued to her tits right now. He's clearly on the friends-to-lovers path with her, so I'm going to get him that gig in London.

It benefits everyone.

Rufus adds a new line to his resume. Piper thinks I'm the hero and I don't have to look at his dick anymore.

Win. Win. And win.

"You would do that for Rufus?" Piper's gaze slides over me. "That's an incredibly generous thing to do."

It's not. It's a blatantly selfish thing to do, but I have no shame where this woman is concerned.

"She's right." Rufus wraps his arm around Piper's shoulder. "You're a better guy than I thought you were."

Considering the fact that I want to snap his arm in two, I'm not going to win any awards for goodwill. The sooner Rufus is out of town, the better.

"I'll talk to Gabriel tomorrow." I gesture toward the studio door and the clear path that I want Rufus to take. "If I need to talk to you, I'll get your number from Piper."

Right before I delete it from her phone forever.

"You'll make it happen, right?" His thick blond brows lift. "You're my ticket to London."

I'll be whatever I need to be to get Piper alone. "I'm taking Piper home now. Keep your phone close, Rufus."

He pats the back pocket of his jeans. "I'll keep it with me twenty-four seven. You'll get by without me, Piper? You'll find another model?"

Brushing her hair back from her shoulder she moves away from him and comes closer to me. Her eyes scan my face before she looks over at Rufus. "I'm good, Rufus. If Griffin can make this happen, this is the chance of a lifetime."

If I can make it happen?

It'll happen. By this time tomorrow, Rufus will be packing a bag for his trip across the pond.

Chapter 29

Piper

I've been debating whether to invite Griffin up to my apartment since we got in the Uber outside the studio. He called for it while I locked up and said goodnight to one of the students who was waiting outside for her ride.

Once we were in the car, the driver started talking about his favorite New York City landmarks. I sat quietly, but Griffin jumped right into a conversation with him. He tossed me a wink when the driver told him that he could recommend some of the best restaurants in Manhattan. It was obvious that he labeled both of us as tourists even though Griffin kept telling him which route to take to get to my apartment the quickest way possible.

I slide out of the car once Griffin exits on the sidewalk. I look up at my building, wishing I had taken a few minutes before I left for work to tidy up. I wasn't expecting any company since the only person who has seen the interior of my place since I moved in is Jo and she doesn't care if it's not in immaculate condition.

"Do you want me to come up?" Griffin straightens his coat.

I study his face. There's no reason for me not to jump at the chance to sleep with him. I've been trying to convince myself that sex with Griffin will distract me from my career, but it won't.

He'll go to work tomorrow. I'll do the same.

We'll see each other in class on Wednesday and if things get awkward, I know he'll quit.

"I'd like that." I gesture toward the front door of the townhouse. "I hope you don't mind the stairs. The elevator hasn't worked since I moved in."

He glances at the building. From the exterior, it looks charming and elegant. It's a pre-war building with a red brick façade but that's where it's allure ends. The foyer has cracked floor tiles, peeling wallpaper and the pungent odor of mold.

"I can handle a few flights of stairs. "He takes my hand to lead me toward a night I sense will be burned into my memory for a very long time.

***

Griffin removes his tie before he takes another sip of the red wine I gave him when we first arrived. I bought the bottle yesterday with the intention of splitting it with Jo since she mentioned wanting to order pizza again one night this week.

I was tempted to go to my bedroom to change my clothes but I don't want to assume anything by getting more comfortable.

"Do you like living here?" He gazes around the living room. "I used to live two blocks over. The neighborhood is great."

The small talk is welcome. My hands have been shaking since I unlocked the door to my apartment. I thought the wine would help calm me down. It hasn't yet.

"So far it's been great." I place my wine glass on the distressed wooden coffee table. "It's pretty quiet and I feel safe here."

That's a bigger deal to me than I'll willingly admit. After what happened with Marco, I double and triple-checked the locks on my door every night before I went to bed. I even slept with most of the lights on for a week after the robbery.

I've been able to let go of the anxiety and now that I know that Marco will be facing a policeman tomorrow, I'll sleep like a baby tonight, unless Griffin has other plans for me.

I feel a blush creep up my neck, so I bow my head and look at the area rug that covers the hardwood floor.

"You saved Marco's life tonight." The wine in his glass sloshes as he places it down on the table next to mine.

I brace my hands next to me on the sofa as I look at his face. "You weren't seriously going to kill him."

He huffs out a laugh. "Not kill, but I would have given him shit before I dragged him down to the police station by the hair on his balls."

"There's a visual I don't want to have stuck in my mind. " I shake my head as I giggle. "If I never see that man again, I'll be happy."

He leans back on the sofa. "What he did to you was fucked up."

I nod. "It was. The entire night was a mistake. I picked the wrong guy out of the crowd."

The worn leather of the sofa groans as he moves slightly closer to me. "Don't beat yourself up,

Piper. There's no way in hell that you could have known he's a bastard."

He's right. I couldn't have predicted what would happen that night but I didn't have to hook up with anyone. It was enough that I ventured out to a club alone. That was a big step for me. Once I was there and I had two vodkas with cranberry juice, I made the hasty decision to have a one-night stand.

It was the most spontaneous thing I've ever done.

"I know," I admit with a sigh. "But as I said, there were warning signs and I completely ignored them and went through with it."

"The kiss." His gaze drops to my lips. "You said back at your studio that you can tell a lot from the way a man kisses."

I stare at his mouth. There's no way in hell that he's not an incredible kisser. His lips are shaped perfectly. They're full without being too plump and I can sense how soft they are.

"You want to kiss me," he growls as he moves closer. "Test your theory."

"My theory?" I drag my gaze from his mouth to his eyes.

He moves quickly, bunching my hair in his fist as his other hand circles my waist. "For the record, I fuck even better than I kiss."

With that, his lips crash down on mine.

Chapter 30

Piper

I don't know how it happened, but we're on our feet. Griffin's hand is still in my hair and I'm fisting his suit jacket.

If what he says is true, I'm about to have the best sex of my life.

The man can kiss.

He deepens the kiss with a swipe of his tongue over mine. I control the urge to moan because I want to savor every second of this. I don't want my body's natural impulses to quicken the tempo of what's happening between us.

"Do you want me?" His voice is low and filled with blatant need.

I can feel his erection pressing against me. It's thick and so hard that I could rip open his belt, unbuckle his pants, yank the zipper down and take him inside me with just a push of my panties to the side.

I'm wet. I'm so wet and aroused that I'm already turning the corner toward an orgasm.

I've never felt this needy just from the touch of a man's lips against mine and the taste of his breath.

It's sweet. Peppermint mixed with the red wine laced with him.

I nod because I have no idea how my voice will sound if I try to speak right now.

"Say it, Piper." He bites my bottom lip. "Tell me you want me to fuck you."

Jesus.

I grip his coat tighter. I lick his bottom lip before I whisper, "I want it."

He pulls back from our kiss, instantly leaving me feeling bereft. "Say it. Tell me you want me to fuck you."

I haven't said those words to a man before. I've only ever let my body speak for me. A touch on his chest, a lick on the tip of his cock, a misguided attempt to give a full blow job that never ended with me swallowing anything but my pride.

I haven't wanted the level of intimacy where I could completely let go before, until now.

I rest my head against his chest. "I want you to fuck me."

"Louder." He pulls my hair back, so I have no choice but to look up and into his face. "Say it so I can hear it."

I lick my swollen bottom lip. There's a small burst of pain from where he bit me. It only makes me want him more. I lock eyes with him. "I want you to fuck me, Griffin."

"Your bedroom," he groans as he picks me up, wraps my legs around his waist and carries me down the hallway.

***

My blouse is off and on the floor before I have a chance to think. I don't complain when I watch his hands move around to the back of my skirt to tug down the zipper. I let him slide the material to the floor, revealing the white lace panties I'm wearing.

I'm thankful that I chose matching lingerie today. The white lace bra is the perfect fit for my breasts.

He stares at my body as he grazes his hand over the front of his pants.

"You're so beautiful."

I should thank him for the compliment, but I'm too focused on what he's doing to form any words. He's staring at my breasts, his hands inching up my sides toward my bra.

He lowers his head and kisses me again. This time it's more fevered, his tongue probes deeply into my mouth trying to coax a moan from me. I can't stop it. I give him what he wants when he trails his lips down my neck to the top of my breast.

He yanks the cup of my bra down and my nipple is as hard as it feels. It's aching, needy and when his tongue flicks out to sample it, I grab his shoulder to steady myself.

The clasp at the front of my bra is no match for his deft fingers. He pushes it off before he drops himself to one knee to slide my panties down.

I'm exposed and wet. I know he can see how much I want him. He lowers his mouth to my pussy, his breath breezing over my swollen clit before the tip of his tongue follows the same path.

It's the barest, lightest touch but it almost tears me in half from its intensity.

"Get on the bed." His voice is gruff and low as he stands. "Jesus, I need to fuck you."

My entire body heats when he unbuttons his shirt to reveal a toned chest and sculpted abs. He's magnificent in every way and when he finally bends down to rid himself of his pants and boxer briefs, I can't help but stare.

His cock is thick and hard, jutting up toward his navel.

He reaches down to fumble with his pants pocket, pulling out a condom package before he tosses it on the bed.

"On the bed," he repeats with less patience and more raw need.

I lower myself to the edge until I'm sitting with him standing in front of me.

My desire to taste him takes over and I lean forward, wrapping my hand around the base of his cock before I drag my tongue slowly over the head to steal the drop of come that's been tempting me.

His hands fist back in my hair as he lets out a guttural sound that shakes me to my core.

My mouth is on him quickly, taking him deep, moaning around his silky hot flesh. I lick, suck and stroke him, feeling him harden even more under my touch.

"Yes," he hisses out. "So fucking good."

He steadies the pace, leisurely fucking my mouth while I rest one hand on his thigh, the other still at the root of him, squeezing and stroking, wanting him to gift me with the taste of his release.

"I can't." He pulls back with a half-laugh wrapped around a grunt. "I want to be inside you. I need it."

I need it too.

I wipe my lips with the back of my hand not caring that he's wet from my mouth.

I move backwards up the bed, my eyes pinned to his. He smiles and my breath catches because he's gorgeous and wanting. His gaze stays locked to mine as he rips open the condom package and sheathes himself.

"Your body is amazing." He crawls over me, his thick heavy cock dragging along the skin on the side of my leg, heating a path straight to my core. "I'm going to fuck this sweet little pussy until you scream my name."

My legs fall open from sheer need. The need to feel; the need to be fucked by this man.

He reaches down to slide the tip of his cock over my slit, parting my lips, teasing my clit.

"I'm going to fuck you and then I'll taste how sweet you are." He keeps his eyes on mine as he pushes in, inch by thick inch.

My back bows with his girth. He takes it slow at first, long steady strokes that take me closer to the edge and when his thrusts become deep and intense, I slide my hands from his back to his hair and kiss him hard.

"I'm going to…" I say against his mouth before my words get lost in the orgasm that washes over me.

Chapter 31

Griffin

I carry the washcloth that I found in her bathroom back to the bed. I ran it under warm water so I could soothe her pussy. I took everything I could from her after she came.

I flipped her over, drove my hands into her hips to pin her to the bed and I fucked her hard until we both came.

"Piper?" I whisper her name against her cheek.

She's on her side in the middle of her bed, her brown hair a halo around her face. She's flushed, and her breathing is unsteady.

"I can't move," she says softly without opening her eyes.

I laugh as I kiss her cheek. "Roll over, baby. Get on your back."

She sighs and I can't tell if it's from the sound of my voice or my command. She acquiesces, stretching out her long limbs before she rolls over, revealing every inch of her perfect body.

I lower the cloth to her pussy, sliding it along the sensitive folds, holding it against her tender flesh.

"You're not too tired to come again are you?" I gaze into her vibrant green eyes. Their depth is immeasurable and with the small amount of light being cast from the lamp on the bedside table, her face is captivating.

"Never." She parts her legs even further.

I take it as an invitation and toss the washcloth on the bedside table before I crawl into place, my lips skimming over the fleshy mound before I flatten my tongue against her clit.

She's sweet and wet.

I lick her slowly, savoring the taste and each of the small sounds she makes.

When her hands drop to my hair, I moan against her, sucking the swollen bud of nerves into my mouth.

Her lips circle, coaxing me to keep going. I do. I lick, I suck and when I slide two long fingers into her, she moans loudly, my name wrapped into the sound.

I close my eyes when I feel her tense against me and when she comes, I groan from her release, my need to have more and the feeling that after tonight, I'm never going to be the same again.

***

I left Piper's place after I ate her pussy. I wanted much more. I wanted to slide my cock into her again. I wanted to shoot my load down her throat, but she fell asleep.

I couldn't wake her a second time, so I got dressed, kissed her goodbye and on my way home on the subway, I sent her a text message telling her how much I wanted to see her again.

It might have sounded desperate or edging on pathetic but my cock was essentially driving my every move by that point.

I was still hard when I got home, but I didn't jack off. I couldn't. I'm saving it for Piper.

"Griffin?" Gabriel Foster walks into his office.

I turn at the sound of his voice and wave my hand. "Gabe."

"What are you doing here?" He smiles.

I push myself to my feet. I was directed to sit after his assistant told me he was in a meeting and I'd have to wait if I wanted to talk to him.

I could have done the deed on the phone, but I haven't seen Gabriel in months. Our friendship is solid, but it's limited to fleeting phone calls and the occasional email now that he's preparing for next year's spring lines for all of his collections.

"Because I've missed your pretty face?" I deadpan.

He laughs. He's a good-looking guy although I'm not a judge on how attractive another man is. He's taller than me with dark hair and eyes.

"I've missed you too." He pats me on the shoulder as he passes me on his way to the chair behind his desk.

I sit back down anxious to get this over with. I have another stop to make before I put in a full day at my office, so I need to get Rufus a place in the London fashion week show now.

"So there's this male model named Rufus…" My voice trails when I realize I have no idea what the fuck Rufus's surname is.

"Rufus Jones?"

Jones? Seriously?

I instantly wonder if he's related to Rocco Jones. He's a friend of Dylan's who consistently beat me at poker every week until I bailed on the games.

"Blond, tall, he looks like he should live on a surfboard," I offer.

Gabriel raises a brow while he opens a file folder on his desk. He rifles through a stack of headshots before he tugs one free and turns it to face me. "Is this the guy you're talking about?"

I glance down at a studio shot of Rufus with much shorter hair and a beaming smile on his face. "That's him."

"What about him?" Gabriel leans back in his chair.

"He wants in on that fashion show you're doing in London." I shake my head. How the hell did I end up here pitching Rufus's case? "Have you got a place for him?"

He narrows his gaze. "Is he a friend?"

I huff out a laugh. "No, I wouldn't call him a friend."

"How do you know him?" There's a hint of amusement in his tone.

I scratch the side of my nose. I might as well fess up. Gabriel will get a kick out of it, and with any luck, Rufus will land a job. "I'm enrolled in an art class. Rufus is the model."

That pulls a hearty laugh from Gabriel. It's enough to draw his head back. "You're not taking that nude figure class he's been posing for, are you?"

"I am."

He studies me for a second. "That's a good step forward, Griffin. I'm proud of you."

I swallow past the lump in my throat. I thought he'd take the opportunity to rib me about it, but he's a gentleman, he always sees below the surface.

I shift the subject back to the reason for my visit. "Do you think you can fit Rufus into your London show?"

"If you want him in London, I'll make it happen." He stands and buttons his suit jacket. "Let's meet for dinner next week. Isla's been telling me she has a friend she wants to set you up with."

Gabriel's wife is a charmer and a fierce romantic. She wants everyone to live the same happily-ever-after she's living.

"I'm seeing someone," I say with a smile. "Someone amazing, Gabriel."

His expression softens. "You're full of good news today. I can't wait to meet her. She must be incredible."

"You have no idea." I grin before I shake his hand and head out of his office.

Chapter 32

Griffin

"Can someone call the police?" Marco Tresoni's strangled voice barely escapes past the hand pinned to his neck.

My hand.

As soon as I left Gabriel's office, I headed to Marco's. I know Piper is going to stop at the police precinct to fill them in on who robbed her, but I wanted in on the action.

"This is assault, Kent."

The mention of my surname by the man parading around Manhattan using my identity is enough to make me shove my fist into the wall next to his head.

"You piece of shit," I seethe through clenched teeth. "I know it was you. You're the son of a bitch who robbed Piper and left my card on the floor. You told her you were me."

He laughs. The red-faced clown laughs. "You heard about that? Now, that was some grade A pussy."

My stomach rolls with the mental image of his dick inside Piper. I have to close my eyes to ward it off. "She's on her way to the police station now. You're going down for this."

"I did go down," he hisses back. "If Morgan tasted half as good as Piper, I'd still be married to the bitch."

I'm not Morgan's biggest fan, but there's no place in my world for men who talk shit about women. I squeeze my hand tighter coaxing a stifled sound from his throat.

I look behind me to where three women have gathered to watch me school Marco. They all flash me smiles which I take as reassurance that no one has dialed 9-1-1.

"Why use my name?" I push him harder against the wall. "Why leave my card behind?"

"I didn't plan it." He tries to push me off him, but it's useless. "I stopped at your office a few days before to try and talk reason with you but you were busy. The receptionist gave me your card."

I raise both brows in silent invitation for him to keep talking.

"I wasn't going to use my real name to pick up a woman at that club, so when I felt your card in my pocket, I went with that. Kent. I never told her my name was Griffin Kent."

What the fuck ever.

"You left the card on the floor." I accuse with another crush of my hand around his neck. "Why do that? You wanted her to end up at my office."

"Why the hell would I want that? You'd lead her straight back to me." He shakes his head. "It must have fallen out of my pocket when I pulled the condom out."

It's one excuse after another with this bastard.

"You took her stuff, Marco." I feel my jaw tighten. "You took her wallet and her phone."

"I have a problem." His face turns beet red. "I'm in therapy. Morgan knows."

He has a whole host of problems at the moment. "What problem?"

"I get a rush when I take stuff." His gaze darts to the door of his office. "It's been a compulsion for years."

"Oh my God." One of the women behind me screams out. "Are you the one who stole my wedding ring? Was that you?"

I push him closer to the wall. "Answer her."

He nods, his voice escaping quickly. "I did it. I took the ring, Gloria's tablet, that silver pen that Marilyn got for her birthday."

"You lying bastard." I feel a pair of hands on my arm. "Let me at him. I'll kill the jerk."

"I'm an attorney. I strongly advise against murder." I look down into the warm brown eyes of a woman who is older than me. "Let the police handle it. I'd much rather see Marco's ugly face in a mug shot than your pretty one."

She smiles. "I'll make the call and thank you."

"My pleasure." I loosen my grip on Marco's neck. "This was all my pleasure."

***

"This is my boss." Piper wraps her arm around the shoulder of the woman I met a few weeks ago. "Bridget Beckett. Bridget, this is Griffin Kent."

Bridget reaches out her hand. I take it because it's expected but also because I can see by the look on Piper's face that this moment means a lot to her.

"You're the man who bought Piper's sketch." Bridget smiles warmly as she tugs her hand from mine after a firm shake.

"Sketches," I correct her. "I've purchased several of Piper's sketches."

Piper throws Bridget a knowing glance. "Griffin actually bought some of my sketches to give to Sem Jansen."

"I heard that you arranged that night for Piper. It was such a gracious thing to do."

It was selfish. I wanted to give her a gift that trumped every other gift she's ever received. I believe I did that. "Piper deserved it."

Bridget studies my face before she looks over at Piper. "I feel some tension here. I'm not imagining that, am I? There's more to this than a student and his teacher."

I wait for a beat for Piper to respond, but it's obvious the question took her by surprise. I answer because I want this woman to know exactly what's going on between us. "We're seeing each other."

Bridget's face lights up in glee as her gaze volleys between Piper's face and mine. "Piper, you didn't say anything. Why didn't you tell me?"

Piper tosses me a look before she turns to face her boss. "It's new. It's still really new."

Bridget reaches forward to grab my forearm. "You'll come to the staff dinner at my house with Piper on Sunday."

I look to Piper for guidance but she's staring blankly at Bridget. "I'm on board. Tell me where, when and what I need to bring."

Chapter 33

Piper

I stare at Griffin after Bridget walks away. I'm at work early today. I had so much restless energy after I woke up after spending last night with him.

I read the text message he sent me over and over. He wrote that he had a fantastic night and that he wanted to see me again as soon as possible.

I didn't think that meant that he'd show up at the gallery before lunch.

"You're okay with me going to this dinner thing on Sunday, right?" Griffin presses his lips to my cheek for a soft kiss. "If you think it's too soon for me to tagalong, just give me the word."

I think it's too soon for me to want him there, but I do. I love the idea of meeting the rest of my co-workers with this handsome man by my side. After what we shared last night, I'm ready to spend as much time with him as I can.

"We'll have fun." I run my hand through my hair.

I didn't put any effort into my appearance today. I showered after I woke up and realized Griffin had left. Then I straightened my hair, put on a light touch of makeup and dressed in dark pants and a green sweater.

Since I don't have class tonight, I didn't expect to see him today.

It was a welcome surprise when I turned at the ring of the bell over the gallery door to see him standing there.

"I went to see Marco earlier."

My entire body tenses at the mention of the man who stole my wallet along with a sliver of my pride. I stopped at the police precinct on my way here, but the officer assigned to my case told me that a man had called in very early this morning with a tip on the identity of the thief. I knew that had to be Griffin.

"What did he say?" I ask with a quirk of my brow.

"What could he say?" He attempts a small smile. "He admitted everything. It turns out that you're not the first person he's robbed."

That doesn't offer me any comfort at all. The only thing I feel is compassion for his other victims.

"Will he be arrested?"

He nods. "Today. He'll be booked and released. Depending on how he pleads, you may not have to go to court."

"I hope he pleads guilty." I rest my hands on my hips. "Did you kick him in the groin for me?"

He smiles wolfishly. "Is that what you would have done if you saw him today?"

"That followed by a poke in the eye." I jut my index finger out in the air. "I think he deserves worse, but at least it would be a start."

"I practically strangled the life out of the asshole. It got him to confess and none of the witnesses remember the part about me having my hand wrapped around his scrawny neck."

I carefully study his face trying to decide if he's joking or not. "You're my knight in shining armor."

He looks over to where Bridget is standing by the charcoal portraits. Her attention is focused on the person on the other end of the phone. Her hand is waving wildly in the air as she laughs out loud.

"I'll be your knight in shining armor, as long as I can be your lover too."

Lover. I want that as much as he does.

"Have dinner with me tonight," he goes on. "I know a great Italian restaurant that's not far from your apartment. We can share a plate of spaghetti before we head back to your place for dessert."

"It's a date," I whisper as I move closer to him. "You'll text me the time and place?"

"I'll do that. I'll think about fucking you all day," he rasps.

My gaze darts to where Bridget is still engrossed in her phone call. "I'm at work, Griffin."

"You're wet." His index finger takes a slow path up my arm, lazily drawing small circles over the goosebumps on my skin. "Your nipples are hard. You want me inside of you."

I dip my chin to hide the need that I know is evident in my eyes. "Don't start what you can't finish."

His hand lands on my chin to tip it up until his gaze locks on mine. "I'll finish tonight when I shoot every drop of my come down your throat."

***

"Griffin seems like a great guy," Bridget says when she finishes up her call and approaches me.

I got out the feather duster and went to work near the sculptures after Griffin left. I'm not on the clock yet but I want to help out when I can. "We're having fun."

"I remember that kind of fun." She nudges her elbow into my side. "Dane and I still have a lot of fun, but we have to do it in our bedroom, or the shower. We don't want the boys to catch us."

I smile at the mention of her husband. She's showed me a picture of him last week in his uniform. He's a fireman and judging by the way she smiles when she talks about him, they're madly in love.

"You have the perfect life." I lean into her. "You have an incredible husband, two beautiful boys and you run this place."

"It's not perfect," she corrects me with a wiggle of her finger in the air. "We have our struggles but we do it together. That's the key. I never bail on Dane and he'll never bail on me. We're in it until one of us takes their last breath. If it's him, mine will be a minute later."

I've never thought about marriage, kids or a love that is so deep that others can hear it in your voice and see it on your face.

I already know that when I meet Dane, I'll see how much he loves his wife.

"Did you know he was the one right from the start?"

She turns to face me. "I thought it was going to be a one-night stand."

I'm surprised. I imagined that it was love at first sight and the story would revolve around some huge romantic gesture on his part that swept her off her feet and into his heart.

"Obviously it's lasted longer than a night," I joke.

"We both knew that night that our connection was unlike anything either of us had ever felt before." She cups her hands together and holds them against her chest. "He broke up with his girlfriend minutes before we met. The next night we were in bed together."

My brows perk. "Did you think you were his rebound?"

She nods. "I did, but he made me feel that I was his everything pretty early on. He's the one who encouraged me to pursue art as a career. He believed in me right from the start."

"The world is in his debt." I glance to where her portraits are hanging. "You're sharing that gift with all of us."

"I'm sharing my life with the man of my dreams." She tilts her head. "I think the man of your dreams is Griffin Kent and one day, you'll be telling me that yourself."

"We barely know each other," I insist. "It's way too early to start talking about forever."

"Mark my words, Piper." She rests her hands on my shoulders. "Griffin looks at you the very same way Dane looked at me right after we met. That man is falling fast."

Chapter 34

Piper

"Christ, Piper. Your fucking mouth."

Technically, Griffin should be saying that he's fucking my mouth, but since I dropped to my knees on my apartment floor and unbuttoned his pants, he hasn't formed full words.

It's been mostly grunts, moans and the occasional hiss of air between his teeth.

I look up into his face. His hair is a mess from where I tugged it when he kissed me in the restaurant. We sat in a corner booth, with one plate of spaghetti to share between the two of us.

We barely ate because both of us were in a rush to get back here.

I inch back until only the wide crown of his cock is in my mouth. I trace circles over the tip with my tongue while my hand strokes the thick length.

"I swear to fuck this is the best thing I've ever felt."

My core aches with those words. I've done this for men before, but it was always a prelude to more. With Griffin I want this to be everything for him. I want him to come.

I brace my hand against his thigh as I suck him deeper, working on a swallow.

"Holy shit," he pants. "Do that again."

I do it again, twice. I'm gifted with a litany of curse words from his lips.

I suck harder, quickening the pace as his hips circle in rhythm to my movements. He takes over, slowing me with his hands in my hair as each pump takes him deeper.

My eyes burn, tears well in the corners from the sheer girth of him.

"Tap my thigh if you need a break, baby," he whispers.

I won't. I can't.

I glide my hand up and down the shaft, smoothing my tongue over the crest.

He thickens beneath my touch. I want to reach down and touch myself. I could come just from the taste of him and the look on his face.

I shake my head when he starts to pull back and as I feel the tension rush through his body I close my eyes to ready myself for his release.

It's hot, thick and as it hits the back of my throat, he calls out my name in a voice laced with desire.

***

"That was one of the most incredible experiences of my life." He's in my kitchen now, his dress shirt unbuttoned, his pants still hanging open and his semi-hard penis in view. He looks like a man who couldn't wait to fuck.

I like that. I love knowing that I'm the woman he was so desperate for.

I reach for the glass of water in his hand. I down half of it before I refill it under the tap. "Mine too."

"I'm staying the night," he announces as he slides the shirt from his shoulders. "We're taking a shower and then I'll return the favor."

"It wasn't a favor." I move closer to him, cupping his cheek in my palm. "I did that because I wanted to. I don't expect anything in return."

His eyes meet mine. They're fiercely focused, stirring with something I can't place. "If I was too rough, I need you to tell me. I know it's…" he looks down at his now hard cock. "More than a mouthful."

"It's perfect." I brush my lips over his as I slide my hand down his chest. "It was my first time."

"Your first blow job?" Confusion furrows his brow. "You're shitting me, Piper."

I kiss him again, harder this time before I whisper softly against his lips, "No, that was my first time tasting a man. Swallowing. I've never done that."

His hands dart to my face. He tilts my head slightly so he can look directly into my eyes. "What a gift. Jesus. What a gift you gave me."

I feel like I'm the one who received the gift from him. He was vulnerable in those moments right after he came. He shook, so I stood and wrapped my arms around him while I pressed my lips to his chest.

"Take me to bed, Griffin. It's my turn to come."

He kisses me softly. "This thing between us, you feel it too? It's good, right?"

I stare into his intensely blue eyes. "It's good. It's really good."

Chapter 35

Griffin

I stare at Piper while she's asleep.

We went at each other after we showered together. I threw her on the bed, crawled between her legs and ate her through two intense orgasms.

Just as she was falling from the high, I sheathed my cock and ordered her to ride me. She did, wildly. The scratches on my chest are proof of the depth of what she felt.

When I felt her pussy grip me during her last orgasm, I shot my load. It was too good, too much, and more powerful than anything I've ever felt before.

"Griffin?" Her voice is throaty and deep as one of her eyes flutters open. "Are you awake?"

I haven't slept.

It's close to four a.m. now, but sleep won't find me. I'm too amped up on the thrill of being with her.

"Go back to sleep." I inch closer to wrap my arms around her. "You can still get in a few more hours before our morning fuck."

She laughs softly, her other eye popping open. "You have more stamina than anyone I've ever met. Sooner or later your cock has to give out."

I reach down to squeeze it. It's already hard and aching for her. "I could go again right now."

Her lips trail kisses over my jaw. "Close your eyes for an hour or two. Dream about me before we make love again."

Make love. That's a first for me.

When I've been with women in the past, it was always a quick fuck or a short-term relationship. I've never understood why some guys feel the need to seek out a woman to bond with.

I can see the appeal now. This woman changed my entire world when she showed up in my office that first day. I knew I had to know her, touch her, have her.

I glance down at where she's tucked herself into the curve of my body. Her hands are fisted together next to her face, her tits are pressed against my chest and her leg is bent over mine as she lulls herself back to sleep.

I try to will my erection away as I close my eyes and feel the instant sensation of peace washing over me.

Next to this woman is where I belong.

***

"You're leaving?" Piper rolls over in her bed to look at me.

I've been awake for the better part of thirty minutes. I expected to sleep for an hour or two with her in my arms, but my body apparently needed more. When I finally woke it was near nine a.m. and after a quick shower and a call to Joyce to tell her to push my first appointment of the day back, I'm dressed and ready to head to my place to change my clothes and grab a case file from my home office.

"I need to get to work." I lean down to kiss her softly.

She smells incredible. It's a heady mix of her perfume and sex.

She kicks the lightweight blanket that's been covering her body off. I know I shouldn't look down, but I do. She's a beautiful woman. Every inch of her is utter perfection.

How in the hell am I supposed to walk away from this to go to work?

"In the middle of the night you said something about morning sex," she purrs. "I've never had that. Can you teach me?"

Sexy little siren.

"I'll teach you everything I know," I whisper into a soft kiss on her lips. "This is going to be for you. All for you, Piper."

I don't bother undressing because I don't want to waste a second of time with her.

I slide down the bed, parting her legs, revealing the soft brown curls above the seam of her pussy.

I take my first taste with a swipe of my tongue over her clit. She squirms. "Griffin, I'm already wet."

She is. She's wet and ripe. Her flesh is still swollen from last night.

"Relax, beautiful." I tenderly rest one of her legs over my shoulder before I do the same with the other. "Lay back and enjoy this."

Her hips circle on the bed as I dive in, eating her with a fury, aching for more but knowing that her taste will linger on my lips for the rest of the day.

Chapter 36

Piper

"I'm going to miss you, Piper." Rufus drops the towel around his waist. "Not only did you give me a shot at modeling for you, but you're the reason I'm going to London for fashion week."

I don't look down. I've never been interested in Rufus's body beyond the fact that it's been a tool for me to use to teach my students about the human form.

"You have Griffin to thank for London," I point out looking over at his empty stool.

I was hoping he'd come to class early today. After he ate me to an orgasm yesterday morning, he left my apartment in a rush.

Since then, we've only had three short text message exchanges. He's been overloaded with work the past two days and I've not only been working, but I've been searching for a model with the same body type as Rufus to take over his spot next week.

So far, I haven't found anyone.

"I have a friend who is interested in this gig." Rufus rakes his hand through his blond hair. "I know you probably have a bunch of guys waiting in line, but he's a lot like me. I think he'd do a great job."

It's exactly what I needed to hear today. I don't hesitate at all. "Are you serious? I've been hitting brick wall after brick wall trying to find someone."

"My buddy, Cameron, will do it." He looks over to where his clothes are sitting on a table. "I can shoot him a text right now to arrange for us to meet him after class for a beer. You can check him out and see if he'll work for you."

I glance at Griffin's easel. He's still not sitting on the stool behind it.

My first choice would be to hang out with him after class, but I won't have a class to teach next Monday if there's no model on the stage. I could switch it up and offer the position to a woman but the course is already half over and my students are making great strides in perfecting their interpretations of the male form.

"Set that up," I say excitedly. "I'll see if Griffin wants to join us once he's here."

Rufus smiles. "Good idea. I can buy the suit a beer to thank him for getting my ass to London."

***

I stare at my still full wine glass. I ordered a red wine once Rufus and I sat down after arriving at this bar down the street from the gallery. His friend is running late, but he's not the man I'm anxious to see.

Griffin never made it to class and even though I've sent him two text messages since we arrived here, I haven't heard anything from him.

I try to shake off the sense of impending doom in my stomach. I didn't think he was the type of man to take a woman to bed only to ghost on her the next day. I want there to be a logical explanation for why he didn't show up tonight. I need there to be because I'm starting to develop feelings for him.

"Cameron!" Rufus jumps to his feet when a man who resembles him walks through the door. "Over here, man."

I smile even though anxiety is buzzing through my veins. I have to shake off Griffin's absence so I can secure a new model for class.

"This is Piper." Rufus taps me on the shoulder. "She's the artist I've been telling you about."

Rufus's friend approaches quickly with his a leather portfolio tucked under his arm. He's the same height as Rufus and from where I'm sitting his body type is identical too.

"It's good to meet you." He stretches out his hand toward me. "Rufus has told me a lot about you. I've seen your portraits online. I'm in awe of the work you're doing."

It's a compliment that I don't put a whole lot of weight in. He's looking for a job.

I shake his hand quickly, motioning for him to sit across from me. He does. Rufus takes the seat next to me sliding his bottle of beer across the table until it's in front of him. "Did Rufus bring you up to speed on what I'm looking for?"

It's a diplomatic way of asking if he's comfortable being nude in front of a group of strangers.

Cameron opens the portfolio in his hand and slides out several black and white pictures.

"These are some of my most recent nude shots." He pushes them toward me. "I did a shoot with a photographer a couple of months ago. These were for his show in Los Angeles."

I glance down at them. The shots themselves are gorgeous. The lighting that was used adds a distinctive touch to the images. He's perfect. I look up at him. "These are beautiful."

He gives me a bright smile. "I'm available on Monday and Wednesday evenings. Rufus told me the schedule. The pay is more than generous and I can start on Monday."

He's covered everything I was about to say. "I'll need your contact information so I can send you a copy of the contract I have the models sign. If you're good with the details of that, we'll hit the ground running on Monday night."

Rufus motions for a server standing next to the bar. "I'll grab you a beer so we can celebrate, Cameron. They guy who got me the London job was supposed to be here too, but he bailed on class tonight." He turns his attention to me. "I'll need his number from you, Piper. I want to send him a text to thank him."

I almost tell him not to hold his breath waiting for a reply as I scan my phone's screen to see that nothing has arrived from Griffin yet.

I push past the sudden knot in my stomach to paste a smile on my face. Worrying about what's going on with Griffin won't propel my life forward. I have to stay focused on my career. It's the only thing I can count on.

Chapter 37

Piper

I've never considered myself the type of woman to chase a man down, but that's exactly what I'm doing right now.

Griffin finally got back to me late on Wednesday evening to apologize for skipping class. His text was cryptic and curt.

Griffin: Sorry. Something came up.

I don't like games, so I didn't see the value in waiting hours to respond. I typed out a message and hit send almost immediately.

Piper: I'll give you a private lesson whenever you want. Maybe you can try drawing me nude.

I admit I was deflated when I got nothing back until yesterday afternoon.

His response wasn't what I was expecting.

Griffin: Meet me for coffee tomorrow morning. The Roasting Point on 7th Ave at 9 a.m. We need to talk. It's important.

I didn't reply to confirm until hours later because I was focused on helping Bridget plan her next course outline. She's launching a special class next month at an extended care facility in Brooklyn. It's a pro bono deal for the residents of a home where the mom of one of best friends used to live.

It's admirable and I told her that I'd gladly do whatever I can to help out.

"Piper?" Joyce's voice tugs me from my thoughts.

I've been sitting in an uncomfortable chair in the reception area of Kent & Colt for the past ten minutes. I asked Fiona if she could let Griffin know that I'm here to see him. She didn't.

Instead, she called Joyce and left her a message to come to reception when she was free. She explained that there was a note on her desk when she arrived an hour ago telling her to direct all Griffin's calls to Dylan.

After Fiona left to grab a coffee, I started to wonder if I should follow her out. I was about to, but now that Joyce is here, I may get my chance to see Griffin face-to-face since he didn't show at the café.

I waited fifteen minutes before I sent him a text asking where he was. When another thirty minutes had passed with no word from him I came here expecting to find him knee deep in someone's marital drama.

"How have you been?" Joyce walks toward me with a stack of file folders in her hands. "Griffin told me that Marco Tresoni was the jerk who robbed you. I'm not surprised. I knew something was off with that guy when he kept showing up unannounced to see Griffin."

"I'm fine." As thankful that I am that Marco has finally been caught, he has nothing to do with why I'm here. "I'm trying to reach Griffin."

"You and me both." She sets the folders on the reception desk with a thud. "He's out of touch at the moment."

"Out of touch?" I furrow my brow. "What does that mean? Isn't he in his office? I only need two minutes with him. I promise I'll be in and out in a flash."

That lures a soft smile to her lips. "I take it this isn't about your art class?"

I have nothing to hide from this woman. I don't know if Griffin tries to keep his relationship status under wraps here at work, but Joyce doesn't seem like the type to gossip. "We've been seeing each other."

Her brows pop up in surprise. "Really? That's great news, Piper. He needs a woman like you in his life."

I like that she thinks so. I sense that they're close even though he's her boss. "I need to talk to him about something personal."

She motions for me to follow her. "He'll tell me I'm fired for disturbing him, but it's a lie. If you two are dating, I know he'll want to see you."

I stand up and adjust the row of buttons on the red blouse I'm wearing before I shove my hand into the front pocket of my jeans.

"You look beautiful." Joyce turns back to me. "Let's go find that man of yours."

***

"I don't know what to say." Joyce scratches her chin as she gazes down at Griffin's desk. "Typically when he tells us not to disturb him, he's in here working on a case."

I glance back toward the hallway. "Maybe he just stepped out for a minute? Could he be in one of the other offices?"

"He's not." A male voice turns me around.

It's Dylan Colt.

"Where is he?" Joyce calls from behind Griffin's desk. "This is the Campbell file here. He's scheduled to be in court this afternoon for the preliminary hearing."

"He asked for a continuance." Dylan steps into the office. "His attention was needed elsewhere."

What the hell does that mean?

I wait for him to offer more, but he doesn't, so I ask for clarification. "Will he be in at all today?"

"No," Dylan says curtly. "I don't expect him until Monday at the earliest."

It's Friday. He's skipped out on his practice until next week?

My fingers flex with unwanted tension. "So his attention was needed on something other than work?"

"It's a personal matter." Dylan clears his throat. "I'll let him know you're looking for him when I speak to him."

"I can always take down a message for him." Joyce rushes to my side with a pad of paper and a pen in her hands.

I don't know why this is grating on my last nerve, but it is. Griffin and I spent a couple of fun nights together, it's not as if we pledged our unending devotion to each other.

Maybe I should have read between the lines of his last message to me. *'We need to talk'* suddenly seems ominous considering the fact that he's checked out of his life for a few days.

I shake my head in frustration and my eyes catch on the wall across the office. My sketch is gone. All that's left is a nail where the frame once was.

"That's not necessary," I say without directing my words at either of them. "I'll talk to Griffin myself when he decides to get ahold of me."

It sounds petulant. I'm embarrassed. I rushed down here expecting to find the man who asked me if I felt the same things he did the other night. Now, I'm leaving unsure if I'll see him again.

Chapter 38

Piper

"It's good to meet you, Piper." Dane Beckett hands me a glass filled with lemonade. "My wife can't stop talking about you."

I look over to where Bridget is pushing one of her boys on a tire swing.

She lives in a quaint house in Queens with Dane and her two sons, Seth and Shayne. It was an easy ride on the subway here.

"She's been really supportive," I offer back. "She's a wonderful person."

"She's the best," he agrees with a nod of his chin. "She said you were bringing someone with you. Are they on their way?"

I wish. Bridget didn't ask about Griffin when I first arrived. She didn't need to. I had sent her a text early this morning telling her that I'd be arriving solo. She replied with a sad face emoji. It was appropriate because it was exactly how I felt at that moment.

I finally got a text from Griffin on Friday afternoon. It was to the point.

Griffin: Sorry about the café. I'll be in touch next week.

I didn't bother to reply.

"He can't make it," I don't elaborate before I change the subject. "Bridget says you're a fireman. That has to be an intense job."

He studies my face with his deep brown eyes. "Some days I love it. Other days I swear I'm ready to quit, but it's in my blood. I can't walk away from it."

I can sense that about him. Bridget has told me how loyal he is to the people he loves. It's the same with his job.

"Did you get a chance to meet everyone?" He motions to a small patio area set up near the swing set.

I glance over to where my co-workers have all gathered. I spoke to them briefly before I excused myself to use the washroom. They were all introducing me to their significant others. I needed a break so I sought out the place I knew I could be alone. After I adjusted the belt on my pink sundress, I came back out here to find Dane waiting for me.

"I did." I wave to Bridget when she lifts her hand toward us motioning for Dane and me to leave the deck to join her. "Callan seems like a blast."

Callan Kincaid leads a beginner sculpture class on Saturday afternoons. He's older than I am with a passion for art that rivals my own. After he told me who he was, he launched into a longwinded account of his journey from a small boy who used modeling clay to create animal figures to an award-winning sculptor.

Kristy Molten and Carol Rempel, the other two teachers here, rolled their eyes behind his back, as he waxed poetic about his accomplishments.

"He's full of himself," Dane whispers before he takes a drink from his glass of lemonade. "There's no mistaking his talent, but he's been a handful for Bridget. He thinks he's cruising at the same speed as

Beck. It wouldn't hurt if someone knocked him down a notch or two."

I laugh, enjoying how easy it is to talk to Dane. "My very first art teacher told me that there's greatness in humility."

"That person was a genius." He starts to move toward the three wooden steps that lead down to the yard. "Let's go join the party. Beck and his family will be here soon and then I'll grill some burgers and ribs."

It's an ideal way to spend a Sunday afternoon. The only thing that would make it better is if I had some understanding of where Griffin went and whether there's a chance for anything between the two of us in the future.

***

"Ribs and potato salad?" Jo peeks into the plastic containers that Bridget filled for me before I left her place. "This is a feast, Piper. You're going to join me, aren't you?"

I pat my stomach. "I already ate. My boss packed that up for me to give to you."

Bridget told me to give the food to Griffin because she's optimistic that he'll show up at my place within the next day. I know better, so instead of letting the food go to waste, I brought it over to Jo's.

"I'll eat half now and you can take the rest for lunch tomorrow." She moves toward the cupboard above her sink to retrieve a plate. "I haven't had ribs in a long time."

I settle in on a chair next to her kitchen table. "They're delicious. Dane, my boss's husband, grilled those."

"You were over at their place today?" She forks two ribs out of the container along with a heaping serving of the oil and vinaigrette-dressed potato salad.

"Bridget, my boss, has a staff party at her place every couple of months." I watch as she snaps the lids back on the containers. "It's a potluck. I brought cupcakes. I would have saved one for you, but those disappeared in a flash."

She picks up a rib and takes a bite. "That boy knows how to cook. These are delicious."

They are. I ate until I couldn't fit another bite of food in my stomach. I relaxed as soon as Beck arrived with his wife, Zoe, and their son, Vane.

Zoe's a lawyer, but she's nothing at all like Griffin. She's laid back and it's easy to tell that her number one priority is her husband and child. We spent most of the afternoon talking about being transplanted New Yorkers since she's originally from Philadelphia.

"Did your friend go with you?"

My head snaps up at that comment. "My friend?"

"Griffin," she clarifies with a wink. "Lana's friend. I guess he's technically more than a friend to you. He was leaving your place the other morning at the same time I was heading out."

I bow my head. "I don't know what he is."

"Handsome." She laughs. "You can't deny that."

I look up and smile. "He's very handsome. He's also confusing. I have no idea what's going on with him."

She drops a rib bone on her plate before she starts on the potato salad. She eyes me up as she chews. "I'm great at decoding men. I've been married three times."

My brows shoot up. "Three times?"

I don't see how that qualifies her as a male decoder since it obviously hasn't worked out for her with the men she's chosen to devote her life to.

"The first two died." She sighs heavily. "One from cancer, the other in an accident at work."

"I'm sorry," I offer sincerely.

"The third was the love of my life." She trails the fork through the salad on her plate. "Someone else was the love of his life. He didn't figure that out until he put a ring on my finger."

I want to offer words of comfort, but I don't have any. Her past explains the sadness that I always see in her eyes.

"That's water under the bridge." She rolls the fork in the air. "Let's get back to you. What's going on with you and Griffin?"

I shrug as I move to get a glass of water. "We had a great night together. Then we made a plan to meet for coffee, but he stood me up. I went to his office to get an explanation."

"What did he say?" She glances over her shoulder to where I'm standing near the kitchen sink.

I sigh as I run the tap to cool the water. "He wasn't there. The partner at his law firm said he had to take care of something personal."

"That's it? Griffin didn't call you to explain why he was a no show?"

"He sent me a text." I shake my head. "All it said was that he was sorry and he'd be in touch. I didn't respond."

"Good girl." She turns back to her food. "Don't chase any man, Piper. Let him fight for you. I learned that lesson the hardest way possible."

I don't expand on the conversation. I won't. It's digging up painful skeletons of her past.

Jo's a reminder of what can happen when you invest your heart in someone too fully. I started falling too hard and too fast for Griffin Kent. I have to forget about him since it's obvious that I'm way more invested in this than he is.

Chapter 39

Griffin

"I'm a dick." I scrub my hand over my jaw, trying to relieve the tension I've been feeling for days.

Piper's shoulders stiffen before she turns on her heel to face me.

Her eyes lock on mine. "I'm in full agreement with that. Why are you here?"

She's pissed. How the hell can I blame her for that? We fucked and then I fled. It wasn't intentional. My family's world fractured, again, and I went to pick up the pieces.

"I'm sorry," I offer. It's so fucking weak. It can't undo what she must be feeling.

I've ghosted on women. Hell, it's been years since I've done it but I remember the guilt that came with it. I saw the impact of my actions in the face of a woman I fucked. She wanted more, but I gave her nothing but silence. I ran into her one night at a club a month after we'd spent a weekend together.

She gave me a piece of her mind along with a stinging slap across the face. It woke me up.

I've tried my best to respect women since then but that went to hell when I took off last week.

"You should go." Her hand shakes as she points at the door of the gallery.

She didn't notice me when I first walked in because she was too engrossed in a conversation with a woman about one of her sketches. When the woman nodded, I saw Piper's face light up.

That expression didn't waver as she rang up the purchase. It shifted the second her gaze caught mine.

I want to be the person who brings that joy to her life. I want to make her feel that valuable with every breath, but I stole her trust. I see it in her body language. I hear it in her voice.

"Let me explain." I close my eyes. "I should have called to tell you I couldn't make our coffee date. It was wrong of me to leave you sitting there."

She bows her head. "There's nothing to explain, Griffin. We had fun. It's over now. End of story."

This is not the end of our story.

"I skipped class last Wednesday because of work," I start with a heavy exhale. "I was stuck in a meeting with a client that ran for hours. It didn't wrap up until midnight."

She shakes her head slightly. "Sure."

"The next day you sent me that message about drawing you nude." I close my eyes, picturing her body in my mind. "Jesus, Piper. That set me off. I had to jack off in the bathroom at the courthouse. The clerk came looking for me since we were already back in session."

Her blank expression doesn't waver. She doesn't want these crumbs. She wants to know why I dropped off the face of the fucking earth for four days.

I suck in a deep breath. "My family needed me, my brother..."

"You have a brother?"

That question is always a punch in the gut. It's easy to answer yet I can never form the right words, so I respond the only way I know how. "Draven. I spent the weekend with him."

Her expression softens. I can see a million questions in her eyes, but she asks the obvious one. "Is he alright?"

Draven is fine. As fine as a man can be who has to raise a daughter on his own while working long hours. "He'll be alright."

I know she wants to know more, but she doesn't push. "What did you want to talk about at the coffee shop? You said it was important in your text."

It felt important at the time. I wanted to tell her about a conversation I had with Sem about her work. He's impressed.

That can wait now. Repairing the damage I've done to our connection can't.

"Can we talk after class tonight?" I want her alone, and in my arms when we talk. I can't do it here when a customer can walk in at any moment.

"Are you coming to class?" A small smile tugs on the corners of her lips. "I thought you might have given up on that."

"I don't give up when I want something this badly." I want to lean in and kiss her, but I can't be sure she won't gift me with a turned cheek.

She reads between the lines. She knows I'm not about to give up on her, on us. I want this. Fuck, do I want this.

"I'll see you in class." She moves a step away from me.

"And after class?" I ask hopefully.

"One step at a time, Griffin." She pauses for a second. "Let's not get ahead of ourselves."

It's too late for that. I'm falling for this woman. My heart is taking the lead and now, I'm just along for the ride.

***

Great.

Just great.

Rufus's replacement is a bigger dick than he is… has a bigger dick.

Brenda is thrilled. Me, not so much.

I got here on time for once, and was surprised to see Piper at the front of the class talking to man who at first, glance looked a hell of a lot like Rufus. That was with his clothes on.

Now, that's he stripped and he's standing on the stage at the front of the studio facing everyone, it's obvious that this guy received a gift in life that Rufus never had.

"Holy hell, that thing is enormous." Brenda leans forward on her stool. "It's not even hard. It would rip me in two, but what a way to go."

I glance down at the floor.

I know Piper has to be up there talking to him, but for fuck's sake, why do I have to witness this? "Good evening, everyone." Piper claps her hands together. "I want to introduce you all to our new model. Rufus was called away to London. Lucky for us, we now get to work with Cameron."

"Cameron," Brenda echoes his name in a soft tone. "I've always loved that name."

I glance over at her. She's staring at the man who is now rocking a full-on erection.

Jesus. I thought I was impressive.

"As you can see, for the most part, Rufus and Cameron have the same body type." Piper's eyes flit down to his groin. "For tonight, let's focus on Cameron's upper body."

Cameron gives her a nod before he leans down to whisper something in her ear.

She looks up at him and laughs before she whispers something back.

What the fuck is that?

"Why do all the models want the teacher?" Brenda turns on her stool to look at me. "She's pretty but what has she got that I don't have?"

My heart. She's got my fucking heart.

"Let's get started," Piper says excitedly. "I can't wait to see what you all come up with tonight."

I can't wait until this class is over and I can have Piper all to myself.

Chapter 40

Piper

Class didn't go as well as I'd hoped tonight. That's because Cameron's cock stole the show. Every woman was practically salivating in her seat and all the men, including Griffin, wouldn't look in Cameron's direction.

He has a very large dick.

Before class, he whispered to me that he was feeling a draft.

I whispered back that's why I pay him so much.

Unfortunately, Cameron's not going to get rich taking on side jobs like the one he's doing for me. It's pocket change compared to what he could be making in print or magazine ads.

He's incredibly attractive, but the only man I'm interested in is currently sitting across a table from me, nervously tapping his fingers on his chin.

We're at Jo's diner.

I didn't want to take this conversation to a bar because I would have been tempted to order a drink. Since I haven't eaten much today, I know I'd feel a buzz straight away and I want a clear mind while we talk.

He looks down at the mug of coffee in front of him. "My family went through a rough patch years ago. We're still trying to sort through that."

I thought there would be some small talk before we got to the core of what happened last week, but I'm not complaining. I want him to open up even if we end tonight as just friends. I know that he's a good guy. He has to be if he dropped his entire life to run to the aid of his family.

I'd do the same for my parents if they needed me, so I can't fault him for that.

"Do you want to talk about it?" I offer.

He shakes his head, the corner of his lip twitching. "My mom has these panic attacks, and she's had a heart attack. Sometimes she can't tell what's bearing down on her so she'll call me."

"Which was it last week?"

He purses his lips. "Both. It wasn't a full-blown heart attack but her blood pressure spiked. It was sorted at the hospital pretty quickly."

I breathe a sigh of relief. My dad had a procedure two years ago to clear a small blockage in one of his arteries. It was found during a routine test and the doctor said it was the proactive thing to do. I was still scared, even though I had every reassurance from my dad, my mom and the cardiologist that everything would be fine.

"How is she doing now?" I move to take a sip of coffee.

He follows my movements with his gaze. "She's doing better. She's back at home."

I jump at the chance to know more about his family. "Does she live in New York?"

"Connecticut," he answers quickly. "I drove up with Draven. My brother, Draven, has a truck. He drove me to see her."

He mentioned his brother earlier; my interest is piqued again. "You said that you spent the weekend with him? At the hospital?"

"No." He exhales harshly. "We stayed at my mom's house. Draven has a daughter. She took the trip with us, so we hung out with her and my mom once she was released and back home."

"What about your dad?"

He hesitates briefly before he answers. "My folks are divorced. He dropped out of the picture years ago."

I blink a few times, imagining him with his family. I can't help but wonder what they're like.

"I should have kept in touch with you." He leans back in the wooden chair. "I've always been the glue for my family. They look to me for strength. I don't have time to think when I'm trying to put out their fires."

I see the weariness in his face and I hear it in his voice. There's more to tell. I know there is. He's on the cusp of opening up, but it's too soon. We've only known each other a few weeks.

"I understand," I say softly, genuinely. "I was worried. I was curious too. That's the only reason I went to your office after you didn't show up at the café. I wanted to know what you meant when you said we should talk."

"You were at my office?" His brows perk. "I didn't know that."

I'm surprised that he didn't hear about it from Dylan or Joyce. I told them I'd talk to him myself, but I thought they'd at least mention my visit to him.

"Griffin," I take a breath before I continue, looking for strength. "I got a little freaked out when I was there. Maybe, a lot freaked out."

"Because I wasn't there?"

"No." I shake my head. "My sketch wasn't there. It had been taken down. I thought…"

"Jesus, Piper." He moves forward, his hands reaching across the table to cover mine. "You thought I was done with you? Is that it? I was a no-show for coffee and then you see your sketch is gone. You must have thought I was a no-good asshole who dumped you by ghosting."

My lips slide into a smile. "I would leave out the no-good asshole part, but I did wonder if it was over."

"This," he begins before he tugs on my hands. "This is the best part of my life. I need this. I need you."

I need him too. I want him to mean what he's saying.

"I could have been there for you," I say even though I know the words carry a lot of weight considering the fact that we haven't even defined what we are to one another. "I know this thing between us is new, but I'm a good friend."

"You're a great girlfriend," he corrects me with a wink.

My breath catches in my throat. That's a big step. "I'm your girlfriend?"

"I want you to be," he says quietly. "I mean I feel like we were heading in that direction until I took that left turn and drove this off the track."

"We can get back on track if you promise me something."

"Anything." He squeezes my hands. "I'll promise you anything."

"The next time you take a left turn, make sure I'm beside you. Don't leave me behind."

He gives me a wicked smile. "I'll keep that promise."

I pull back my hand, grateful that this isn't ending tonight. I want more time with him. I want to explore where this is going, what it could potentially be.

"I'll stop by the gallery tomorrow afternoon to buy another sketch." He finishes off his coffee.

"Another one?" I can't mask my grin.

He nods. "I gave the one in my office to mom. I told her the most incredible woman I've ever met drew it."

I dip my chin to hide the emotion I know is in my eyes. "Did she like it?"

When he doesn't answer immediately, I look up to find him with a tear in the corner of his eye. "She loved it, Piper."

Chapter 41

Griffin

My dick is throbbing by the time we get to Piper's place. I haven't touched her since we sat at the table at the diner holding hands. I wanted to kiss her in the Uber on the way over, but she was staring out the window of the car, obviously lost in thought.

I shared what I could with her tonight. There's more, so much more, but I can't throw it all at her at once.

"Do you want anything?" She turns back to me after dropping her purse on her sofa. "I think there might be some wine left."

I shake my head as I stalk toward her. "I'm not in the mood for wine."

Her fingers play with the buttons on the front of her white and green striped dress. "What are you in the mood for?"

"I want to fuck you," I say with no hesitation. "If you don't want that tonight, I'll understand, but I'll still need to jack off while I look at you."

A blush blooms on her cheeks. "You'd do that?"

"Masturbate in front of you?" I slide my hands up her arms, relishing in the way she shivers under my touch.

I look down to where her nipples have furled into tight points under the thin material of the dress. I can tell that she's wearing a black push up bra. I noticed it during class when she stood next to me while she was examining my sketch.

"I'd do anything you want me to." I run my nose along her neck. "If you want to see me pump my cock for you, say the word, Piper."

"It sounds so hot." The words come out in a low moan. "I've never seen that before."

I inch my way up her chin to her lips. I kiss her, deeply. "Where do you want it? The shower or your bed?"

She kisses me now. Her hands tangle in my hair as the tip of her tongue dances with mine. "The shower."

"I want you on your knees when I'm ready to blow," I whisper against her mouth. "I want to watch you swallow every last drop."

"Yes," she purrs. "Yes."

***

I toss my head back as I feel her hand cover mine.

"Oh my God," she whispers against my jaw. "I could come just from watching this."

I pump my dick harder. "Touch your pussy."

"Griffin." Her voice is a breathy whisper. "I can't."

I open my eyes and stare down at her. "Touch your perfect little pussy for me."

Her lips part. I feel her hand leave mine. I look down to watch it travel along her flat stomach before it disappears between her legs.

"I want to see," I barely get the words out. "Spread your legs so I can see."

She takes a step back into the water that's now running tepid. "I'm so wet."

"Fuck, yes." I pump harder, my hand moving steadily over my dick. It's so swollen. I'm closing in on a climax that's going to drop me. I can feel it.

"How can I be this close already?" Her hand moves faster. "I told you I was going to come from this."

I drop my cock and fall to my knees. I have to taste. I need to feel her come against my mouth.

She stumbles when I push her back against the cool wall of the shower and when I flick my tongue against the hot bundle of nerves she loses it. She fucking loses it and as I feel her come apart, I fist my cock, bringing myself to my own intense release.

***

"Slowly, Piper," I hiss out. "Go slow."

She nods. I know her pussy is still tender. After she came in the shower, I tongued her to a second orgasm before I toweled her dry and carried her to bed.

She slept briefly, tossing and turning before finally settling in next to me, her hair splayed across my chest, her shallow breaths whispering over my skin.

I didn't close my eyes. I knew if I did, I'd be lost to the exhaustion that gripped me days ago.

I can't waste a moment when I'm with her.

Once she woke up, I was on her like a man who hadn't eaten a meal in weeks. I licked her from behind before roughly shoving two fingers inside of her. I brought her to the edge, then sheathed my cock and ordered her to ride me.

Her hand fists the root of my dick as she lowers herself onto me. Her eyelids flutter shut. "It's so deep like this."

So fucking deep. I grab hold of her waist, wanting to push her down while I spear up into her. The desperate need to fuck is nipping at my spine, driving my movements. "I have to fuck you."

She reaches up to cup her tits as she takes me all the way. "Not hard, Griffin. Slow for now."

How the fuck can I agree to that?
I close my eyes against the image in front of me. It's not just the beauty of her body. It's her face. It's perfect. Everything about her makes me want to claim her as my own.

She rocks back and forth, using my dick to pleasure herself.

"Use me, baby," I manage to get out between thrusts up and into her. "Use me to make yourself come."

She does and then I take.

I flip her over. My pounding drives bring her right back to the edge and when I come I bite out her name while her pussy grips my cock in her own release.

Chapter 42

Piper

I take the glass of water from him and finish what's left. It's the second that he's brought from the bathroom. The first time he also carried a warm washcloth to the bed and pressed it against my pussy to clean me.

It's felt more intimate this time than the first time he did it.

Our lovemaking tonight felt the same.

I rest the empty glass on the nightstand before I flip the covers back on the bed. "Come here, Griffin."

He doesn't hesitate. He crawls into next to me, tugging my body against his. I can sense immediately when his penis hardens again.

I love that he wants me as much as he does, but I'm spent. I've never come that many times in a row before.

"Do you have siblings, Piper?"

I move slightly, resting my chin on my forearm as I lean into his chest. "No, it's just me."

His hand lightly caresses my still damp hair. "Did you ever wonder what it would be like to have a brother or a sister?"

"Not really." I shake my head. "My cousins have always lived next door to us. Lacey and Doug are their names. We did everything together, so in many ways, they are my brother and sister."

His voice softens. "How old were you when you realized you could draw?"

I tilt my head to the side. "I've always been interested in art, but I think the turning point was in middle school. My art teacher told me that she wanted to enter one of my sketches into a contest."

"Did she?"

"She did. I won first prize. It was a hundred dollars and a professional sketch kit."

"It just took off from there?" He tenderly tucks a piece of my hair behind my ear.

My gaze trails over his face. "It was all I wanted to do. We'd take family trips and I'd bring my sketchpad. My dad would take me skiing and I'd bring my sketchpad. It was always near me. I sketched something every day."

"They say practice makes perfect," he shoots back. "You must have practiced a fuck ton."

"A fuck ton and then some." I wiggle my brows. "Once I started college, I realized that human form was the perfect fit for me. It felt natural."

"You're a natural. Your work is exquisite."

"The first time I showed my dad a sketch I'd done of a male model, he turned beet red." I laugh, remembering my dad's reaction. It caught him off guard. He was used to seeing drawings of the mountains, trees and the occasional face. "He told me it was nice. My mom loved it."

"Have they always supported you?" he pauses to take a deep breath. "Did they ever try to persuade you to take a different path?"

"No," I answer matter-of-factly since it's the truth. My parents have both encouraged me to chase my dreams, whatever they are. "They told me to follow my heart. Art might not be the easiest path to take, but if it's in your blood and bones, you don't have a choice."

He closes his eyes as his legs kick beneath the covers. "I need to get up. I don't feel well."

With those words, he slides my arms off his chest, swings his legs over the side of the bed and he takes off in the direction of the bathroom.

***

"You're welcome to stay the night." I stand to the side as I watch him dress. "I can make us some tea. That usually settles my stomach."

I have no idea if an upset stomach is what chased him to the bathroom or not.

"I felt overheated." He rakes me over from head to toe. I'm wearing a short white robe now.

I put my hands on my hips. "You're not saying it's my fault, are you?"

He laughs at the sound of the jest in my tone. "I'm saying that you're the hottest thing I've ever seen, so it might have a little to do with it."

I step closer as he tucks his tie into the pocket of his suit jacket. "You're feeling better now, right? Do you think it was overexertion?"

"From the fucking?" He quirks a brow. "If I didn't have an early meeting, I'd stay and fuck you against that window."

I look back at the window that overlooks the street. "You'd fuck me there?"

"There or on the floor. We could do it against the wall." He leans down to offer me a soft kiss. "Anywhere, Piper. I don't care where it is, as long as I'm inside of you, I'll be happy."

I rub my legs together. "You know that you're making me want to try all those places, don't you?"

He huffs out a deep laugh. "Make a list of where you want to be fucked and I'll come back tomorrow so we can get started."

I sigh. "I have plans tomorrow."

"Plans?" He adjusts the collar of my robe. "What plans?"

"I'm having dinner with Beck after the gallery closes." The words sound foreign coming from my lips. Never in my wildest dreams could I have imagined that Brighton Beck would invite me to have dinner with him to talk about an art project. When he texted me to ask if I was free, I jumped at the chance.

"He's married, right?" He trails his lips over my forehead. "Tell me it's professional."

"I'm your girlfriend, remember?" I nuzzle into his chest. "We're going to talk about the gallery, I think."

"He seems like a smart guy to me." He strokes the pad of his thumb over my bottom lip. "I'm betting that he's going to give up more space at the gallery for your sketches. They're selling like mad right now."

I playfully slap my hand across his chest. "Because you're buying them all."

"I'll drop in tomorrow to pick out a new one for my office."

"I can't wait." I lean into his kiss. "I'll see you then."

Chapter 43

Piper

I've been thinking about what happened last night since I got out of bed this morning. I headed back over to Crispy Biscuit for breakfast since Jo had slid another envelope under my door.

The message written on this one was to the point.

Be at the diner before 9 a.m.

I showered, and dressed in jeans and a gray T-shirt before I slipped on a pink sweater and my short brown boots. I was out of the door before the clock hit eight-thirty.

"You look like you're thinking about something." Jo refills my coffee as she clears my breakfast plate.

Today the special was two waffles with a side of bacon. I was ravenous after my night with Griffin. I ate every last bite in record time.

"It's Griffin," I confess as I empty a packet of sugar in the mug. "We were together last night."

"I know." She winks as she stirs splashes some cream into my coffee. "We passed each other in the hallway."

"Did you talk to him?" I don't want to seem overly nosy, but there was something off about him after we talked about my early days as an artist.

He was kind and considerate in the moments before he left my apartment, but there was a distance in his demeanor that hadn't been there before.

"We spoke," she says as she reaches to wipe the counter in front of me. "It was passing words about the weather, but he looked sad."

That's not something a woman wants to hear after a marathon fuck session with the man she's crazy about, but it's the confirmation that I needed to hear. "We had a great time, but something changed right before he went home."

"Some men can't handle the emotions that come with sex." She leans her hip against the counter. "It's too intense for them. My first husband cried after sex, every single time."

Griffin wasn't that extreme and it didn't feel as though it was related to sex at all. "I'm not sure if that's what it was."

She rubs the back of her neck with her hand. "You like him a lot, don't you?"

I nod. "He's not my type at all, yet he's everything I could ever want in a man."

"I'm not going to pry and ask about what happened last week and why he bailed on you, but keep that heart of yours safe, Piper." She taps the middle of her chest. "A man's secrets can be hidden behind a handsome smile. When that fades, the truth will come out and it can bite you so hard you'll never recover."

We're sliding back into territory that is painful for her. "Is that what happened with your ex?"

"I saw him the other day." Her voice brightens. "He came in for a coffee. I hadn't seen the man in three years, but there he stood by the door with that look on his face that always caved my chest in."

"Did you two talk?" I take a sip of coffee, biting my lip at the burn of hot liquid against it.

"He said I looked good." She looks down at her T-shirt and jeans. "I said he was still a liar. We laughed and he left."

He took a piece of her heart with him again. It's evident in the faraway look in her eyes.

"Will you see him again?" I ask tentatively. "Did he say he'd be back?"

"I won't be waiting if he does." She leans both elbows on the counter. "After he left, Jerry asked me to a ball game."

I gaze over her shoulder toward the kitchen where the gray-haired cook is hard at work. "Jerry? As in that Jerry?"

"As in the man who always has my back." She glances back at him. "After my ex walked out and I turned around to see Jerry's face, it hit me. It's not about what's on the surface. Jerry's not my usual type, but he looks at me like I'm his everything."

That's how Griffin looks at me.

"I know every last one of Jerry's secrets." She laughs. "They're sad. I get the sense that Griffin's are too. Once you get him to open up, you can carry that pain with him. That's what builds a bond that no one can break."

"Has anyone ever told you that you're wise?" I manage a small smile.

"I've heard it a few times." She winks as she stands upright again. "We'll do pizza on the weekend again? We can talk about our boyfriends and braid each other's hair."

I almost choke on the sip of coffee I just took as I try to quiet an uncontrollable laugh. "You're the best, Jo."

"You're not so bad yourself."

Chapter 44

Griffin

"Dude, put on some pants." I toss my keys on the small table in the foyer of my apartment. "I've already seen too much naked cock the past few weeks."

Sebastian's hand darts down to cover his groin. "Shit, man. I thought you'd be at work."

"I thought you'd be at your apartment." I stalk past him on my way to my home office. "Were you here all night?"

I ask because I crashed as soon as I got home. I dropped my clothes on a chair in my room and hit the sheets. I was out within two minutes.

It wasn't until I woke up in a cold sweat at two a.m that I remembered the conversation Piper and I had about her need to be an artist.

I got out of bed, took a shower and worked until I dressed for my early meeting.

I noticed the door to the guest room was closed, but I didn't think twice about it.

"Brad had his kids last night." Sebastian rounds the corner to my office with a pair of black sweatpants on. His chest is still uncovered displaying the tattoo that covers his shoulder. I fucking hate that thing. It's a reminder of the night he was shot.

"Put on a shirt."

"No shirt." He shakes his head. "You know I don't like hanging around when Brad has his daughters for the night. He only sees them one night a week right now. I want to give him space and time with them."

Sebastian has a heart of gold. When Brad, one of his buddies from work, was going through a painful divorce, Sebastian let him move to the extra bedroom in his apartment. It's a good arrangement until the guy's daughters show up.

Those are the nights when Sebastian uses the key I gave him to crash here. I don't have a problem with it, unless he's walking around in the nude.

"Is there a woman here?" I look past him to the hallway. "I'm not going to stumble on some big-titted blonde on my way out, am I?"

He raises a dark brow. "Once, Griffin. That happened once."

Once was enough.

I came home from work and found a beautiful blonde in my bed.

I'm not the type to turn down a gift, so I undressed while she spoke some language that I couldn't understand. *French, maybe?*

It didn't matter.

My cock understands the language of love.

By the time I was down to my boxer briefs, I could hear Sebastian calling out to her.

It seems '*the first door on the left*' doesn't translate well. She hopped into my bed expecting Sebastian. I almost hopped in right after her expecting a good fuck.

She left before either of us got a taste.

"I don't bring women here anymore." He crosses his arms over his chest. "I'm done fucking random women. I'm too old for that shit."

He's thirty-two.

"You and me both." I pat him on the bicep. "I have a girlfriend."

"The art teacher?"

I turn back to look at my desk. "Piper. Her name is Piper."

"I want to meet her."

I pick up a file folder that I forgot to take with me to my office this morning. "We just started going steady last night so give it a day or two."

He laughs. "Cute, Griffin. So you're off the market? First Julian and now you?"

Julian Bishop, our mutual friend since high school, got engaged to the love of his life, Maya, mere months ago. I made a bet with Sebastian that night that I'd be the last of the three of us to fall in love. I'm headed toward losing that wager.

I pivot to face him again. "I'm not getting hitched, Sebastian. We're hanging out and having fun."

"It's more than that. You've been different since you met her."

I pinch the bridge of my nose. "Fine. I'm falling in love with this woman. I want her but I'm scared shitless that I'll mess it up."

"Why? You think your demons are going to tear the two of you apart?" He inches forward. "You've got to trust in what she feels for you. If you can't do that, you two won't make it."

"I trust her. I told her about my family," I say, leaving out the details of what I shared with Piper.

"Good." He pats me on the shoulder. "I'm glad to hear you're opening up."

I close my eyes. "How is it fair for me to feel this good? I don't deserve it."

"You're allowed to be happy, Griffin. Don't fuck yourself over by thinking you don't deserve a good life."

I don't want to go over the reasons why I've never felt worthy of happiness. Not now. I'm about to go to the gallery to see Piper so I change the subject. "You deserve a good life as much as I do. Have you met Maya's sister yet? Wasn't Julian supposed to set you two up?"

"I haven't met her." He huffs out a laugh. "Maya told her I was NYPD. Apparently, Matilda draws a hard line at dating a cop."

"You'll charm the panties off of her at their wedding." I brush past him. "You know Julian's going to pick me to be the best man, so get ready for that."

"Fuck you," he calls after me. "I'm the best man you know."

He is. He's the one who pulled me back from the brink of despair years ago. I'll never be able to repay him for that.

***

"We have to stop meeting like this." I press up against her from behind. "Feel that? That's what happens the second I see you."

Piper wiggles her ass against my erection. Thank God we're the only two people in the gallery. "I take it that means you're happy to see me?"

"Happy?" I echo her tone. "I'm hard as hell here, Piper. I'd call that happy."

She turns to face me, her brilliant green eyes lock on my mouth. "Kiss me, Griffin."

I'll never deny her a request, so I slide my lips over hers for a sweet, soft kiss. "You look beautiful. You smell fucking incredible and you kiss almost as good as you fuck."

She laughs. "Thank you, I think?"

I arch a brow. "Show me what you've got, baby. I need to be in court in thirty minutes, so this visit has to be quick."

"Oh damn. I was going to offer to blow you in the back room," she pouts.

I look down at my watch. "If you keep talking like that I may have to leave my client to fend for herself in front of the judge."

A laugh bubbles up from her. "I'll let you go this time."

I let her lead me by the hand to the back of the gallery where three of her sketches are now hanging next to Bridget's portraits. "You're taking up more real estate back here I see. Your boss knows what's selling."

Her gaze scans the frames. "Bridget's the best. She offered to give me more space for my work. I jumped at the chance."

I look at the sketches. They're all uniquely beautiful, but one stands out. It's a woman. The angles of her body are compelling. She's been drawn from her side, her hair down around her shoulders, partially obscuring her face. It's a larger piece than the others that I've purchased, but it would look amazing in my apartment.

I point at it. "That one."

"This one?" Her finger skims the edge of the frame. "It's more expensive, Griffin. You don't have to buy it."

"I want to buy it." I inch closer to get a better look. "I want this in my home. You can have it delivered there, can't you?"

"Of course," she answers quickly. "I'll arrange that today. I can have the delivery person call you to confirm the best time."

"I have a doorman." I turn to face her. "He'll hold it until I get home so anytime will work."

"I'll need your address."

I tug my wallet from my pocket before I shove my credit card and driver's license in her hand. "I'll wait here and admire my girlfriend's work."

She laughs. "I'll ring it up and be right back."

I stop her by the elbow before she can move, tugging her closer to me. I press my lips against hers for a deep kiss. "You're everything, Piper. You're becoming my everything."

Her breath races over my skin as she tilts her head back to look into my eyes. "You're becoming mine."

Chapter 45

Piper

"If Bridget wouldn't have given me the chance that she did, I would still be back in Denver teaching art class at a community center." I smooth my tongue over my top teeth hoping to catch any wayward pieces of lettuce that may have settled there.

Beck nods as he chews. "When she first showed me your work, I was impressed. She said she got a recommendation from one of your professors?"

"Sally Dorman." I fork another piece of lettuce but don't bring it to my mouth. It's been tough to eat. I'm too nervous. "She had reached out to Bridget a couple of years ago to purchase one of her portraits and they kept in touch."

"I asked you to come to dinner because I want to talk about your future." Beck rests both his elbows on the table.

I take a deep breath. "What about my future?"

"Each year I do a new artist showcase in Boston." He looks to the table next to us where a woman is eating dinner with her daughter. We were witness to their warm exchange when the daughter arrived.

"I know all about that." I smile. "Last year one of the artists was Newton Castroni. I'd already been following his career up until that point, but the exposure from your showcase made him a household name."

"Newton's incredibly talented." He grins. "He's almost as talented as you."

I don't know if he's teasing me or not. "I don't know what to say."

"Say that you'll be in Boston for the unveiling of your sketches in the showcase."

I stare at his lips. "Can you say that again?"

He chuckles. "Your work is going to be included in the showcase, Piper. Six of your sketches. We'll choose them together."

"No," I shake my head as tears cloud my eyes. "This isn't real."

He reaches to cup my hand in his. "This is as real as it gets. I've already told Bridget. She's on board for giving you the time off you'll need to come to Boston for the set-up. She'll be there too for the unveiling."

"I can't believe this is happening." I cover my face with my hands trying to fight back the rush of pure emotion I'm feeling. "How can I thank you for this?"

"Never stop drawing. This is just the beginning of your career, Piper. The art world has no idea what they've been missing."

***

"You're Piper, aren't you?"

I look at the man standing in the doorway of Griffin's apartment. He's dressed in jeans and a white T-shirt. He has black hair, blue eyes and is definitely not the person I expected to see standing in front of me.

I convinced the doorman to let me surprise Griffin. He was wary at first, but when I told him that I was Griffin's girlfriend and that I had a special gift for him, he agreed to let me come up.

The deliveryman standing behind me holding my framed sketch might have helped my case.

"I'm Piper."

"I'm Sebastian."

"You're the homicide detective." I arch a brow.

He smiles. "You're the artist."

I turn to look back at the man standing behind me. "Griffin bought this today at the gallery where I work. I wanted to surprise him by delivering it myself."

He moves to the side and waves his hand. "Griffin's out for the evening, but please come in."

I heave a sigh as I cross the threshold into Griffin's home for the first time. I never imagined this would be how I'd see the place that he lives. I wanted that to be with him, so I could see his expression as he watched me taking everything in for the first time.

I do just that. I scan the room. It's beautiful and spacious. The furniture is dark leather and weathered wood. The kitchen is open with an island that overlooks the main living space. It's gorgeous and refined, just like the man who lives here.

The deliveryman places the frame on the floor so it's leaning against the wall nearest the door. "We'll take off," I say to Sebastian while he studies the sketch. "Will you tell Griffin I was here?"

He shakes his head. "Stay a minute, Piper."

I look over at the deliveryman. I never bothered to ask his name when he came to the gallery to pick the sketch and me up after my dinner with Beck. I was too caught up in my own thoughts to offer even the simplest courtesy to the man. I reach into my purse to pull out some cash before I shove it into his hand. "Thank you again. I appreciate you helping me with this."

He smiles before he turns and walks out the door, leaving me standing in my boyfriend's apartment wondering where he is.

Chapter 46

Piper

"How long have you known Griffin?" I ask Sebastian as soon as we're alone.

"Forever," he replies quickly. "We've been friends a very long time."

I like knowing that. He's a glimpse into a part of Griffin's life I don't know much about. "Do you know if he'll be home soon?"

"He wasn't here when I got back." He rakes his hand through his hair. "I don't live here. I bunked in the guest room last night and stopped in after work to pick up a few of my things."

I nod. I'm uncomfortable. That has nothing to do with Sebastian. He puts me at ease for some reason.

It feels wrong to be here without Griffin.

"Do you know where Griffin is?" I edge forward on my heels. They're too tight. I thought I'd be able to kick them off and slide into bed with Griffin as soon as I got here.

"At the office. He had a late meeting with a client." He moves closer to the framed sketch. "Griffin told me that you've been teaching him how to draw."

I laugh. "I'm trying to teach him how to draw."

"So that talent doesn't run in the family?"

I pause to take in his words. "I'm not sure what you mean."

He looks over at me, his gaze softening. "You don't know, do you?"

Apparently not since I'm lost back where he said that talent doesn't run in Griffin's family. I stare blankly at him.

"Come with me, Piper." He holds out his hand. "There's something I want to show you."

I slide my hand into his, trusting in his kind eyes and my need to know more about the man I'm falling in love with.

***

Tears stream down my face as I stare at the walls of Griffin's home office. I've never seen anything like this before. It's intense and compelling.

I look to my side at Sebastian. "Are there more like this?"

"Dozens." His hand rests on his chin. "These are the ones that mean the most to Griffin. The rest are packed away in a room at his partner's home. Dylan Colt's place. Griffin goes there sometimes to look at them."

I move closer to the center of the room and turn slowly on my heel, taking it all in. My heart hammers in my chest as I study each brush stroke, every tender detail and the haunting pain that jumps out from each canvas.

"Why didn't he tell me about this? About the person who painted these?"

Sebastian's hand falls to the center of his chest. "It's too painful. There's a story here that's not mine to tell, Piper. I just wanted you to see these so you can understand more about Griffin. I can tell that you care about him. I know he cares about you."

As I scan the paintings again, my eye catches on a square silver frame sitting atop a counter. I squint as I look at the photograph inside of it.

It's a black and white capture of a beautiful light-haired woman. Her hair is blowing in the wind, partially masking her face, but I can see her smile.

I approach the frame, wanting to know who she is and if these haunting beautiful masterpieces are a product of her hand.

I knew instantly when I walked into the room that it wasn't Griffin who created these. The artist is tortured, their inner pain so apparent that it drips from each canvas.

"Who is she?" I skim my fingers over the edge of the frame. "Is she the artist?"

"No," Griffin's strangled voice catches me by surprise.

I turn to see him in the doorway of the room, his hands fisted at his sides, his face devoid of expression.

"Get out, Sebastian." He doesn't look at his friend. "Get the hell out of my house."

"I love you like a brother," Sebastian says calmly. "You need to let her in, Griffin. Let her in."

"Leave," Griffin barks out. "Now."

Sebastian looks to me before he makes his way to the door. He doesn't turn back and when I hear his footsteps fade I turn to face Griffin.

"Who painted these?" I rub my forehead. "Who painted them, Griffin?"

He lowers his head in silence.

"I can see that this is painful," I say softly. "Help me understand."

"Go." He points at the doorway, his hand visibly shaking. "You shouldn't be here. Just go."

"Please," I whisper as I approach him. "Don't send me away. I want to know more. I want to know everything."

"Leave," he repeats. "I want you to go."

I bite back a rush of tears as I walk away from him and the future I thought we'd have.

Chapter 47

Piper

"You look like hell, Piper." Jo scoops me into her arms. "Cry, child. Just let it out."

I do. I knocked on her door as soon as I made my way up the stairs to my apartment. I was going to go straight to bed, but I needed comfort and since Bridget lives in Queens and is likely fast asleep, Jo was the only person I could think of to go to. I'm grateful that she's still awake.

She shuffles us both into her apartment before we break the embrace.

"I'm going to make some tea." She points at her sofa. "You sit down and wrap yourself in that blanket. You're wet and cold."

I didn't care that it was pouring rain when I stepped out of Griffin's building. I just wanted to get away so I rushed to the nearest subway stop. By the time I was on the platform, my dress was soaked through and clinging to me.

I'm not a true New Yorker yet. I don't listen to the forecast to know when to carry my umbrella with me. Hell, I don't even own a fucking umbrella.

I don't belong here. I shouldn't be here. My life in Denver was never this complicated.

"The kettle is on." Jo wraps her arm around my waist to push me in the direction of her sofa. "Kick off your shoes. They look like they're strangling your feet."

I do as I'm told before I sit on the sofa while she wraps a soft blue blanket around my body.

"Lean back and close your eyes for a minute." Her hand brushes across my forehead. "I'll get the tea and be back in a flash."

I nod as I look up. "I miss my mom."

"I know, sweetie." She smiles down at me. "I miss my daughter. She's overseas right now. I think fate brought us together."

I sob. "I think so too."

"I'll take care of you. We'll mend your broken your heart."

I lean back and close my eyes, wishing I'd never delivered that damn sketch to Griffin's place tonight. I saw a part of his life he didn't want me to see and now I'll never understand the pain that lives inside of him.

***

I open my eyes to the low hum of the television. I look over at Jo. She's resting her head in her hands.

"Did I doze off?" I snuggle under the blanket as I glance at the two mugs on the coffee table. One still has a tea bag and liquid in it. The other is empty.

Jo smiles. "You were out for about an hour. I didn't want to wake you."

"I don't think I'll ever see him again," I whisper. "I think it's over."

She runs a hand over her hair pushing it back from her forehead. "What happened?"

I sigh heavily. "I went to Griffin's apartment tonight to surprise him, but he wasn't home. A friend of his was there."

She waits patiently for me to continue.

"His friend took me into Griffin's home office. There were these beautiful paintings there. They're striking. All of them are tones of gray with rolling waves, and hills. There are ghost-like figures and abstract forms. It was gripping. I've never seen anything quite like it before."

"Did Griffin paint them?"

I shake my head. "No. I don't know who did."

I don't bother bringing up the blonde woman in the photograph because I can't fit her into the picture. I have no idea if she's a part of Griffin's life now or if her memory was born in his past.

"I take it Griffin found out that you were in his home office without him there?" Her voice softens. "It upset him, didn't it?"

"He found me in there." I close my eyes to push back my emotions. "He looked so vulnerable, so lost. I just wanted to hold him, but he told me to go."

She clears her throat. "Maybe he wasn't ready for you to see that part of his life."

"I can't change the fact that I saw it." I exhale as I look back at her. "It doesn't change how I feel about him."

"How do you feel about him?"

"I think I love him," I admit.

She moves closer to the edge of her chair. "If you do, find a way to show him that."

"I don't know how." I swing my legs over the side of the sofa until I'm sitting upright. "I feel as though I saw a side of him tonight that I never knew existed."

"You're not talking about the fact that he told you to leave, are you?" She rests her cheek against the back of the chair.

"I know why he did that." I tuck the blanket around my legs. "He felt exposed. I'm talking about the paintings. They are so intense. He has them hanging in his office. They must speak to him in a way."

"Or they remind him of something or someone."

"I wish I knew what or who."

"Give Griffin time, Piper." She lowers her voice. "Let him accept that you've seen a part of his world he obviously wants hidden. He'll come to you when he's ready."

Or he won't. Time will tell and until then, I'll find a way to move on with my life.

Chapter 48

Griffin

"If we weren't partners, I would have fired you days ago." Dylan stalks into my office. "What the fuck is wrong with you?"

Everything. Every fucking thing.

It's been more than two weeks since I found Piper and Sebastian in my home office. I lost it in that moment. My rage over the intrusion was enough for me to send them both out of my life. I haven't spoken to either of them since.

I know I'll mend my friendship with Sebastian in time because we've weathered storms worse than this.

It's Piper that keeps me awake at night.

I miss her. I need her. I wish to fuck she wouldn't have seen those paintings.

It made me feel bare in a way I've never felt before.

I hated it. I crave it now. I want more of it but my fear of her rejection is stronger than anything else so I pushed her away before she could do it to me.

"I broke it off with Piper."

"You what?" He stops short of my desk. "Why?"

I rest my head in my hands. "It was that or I had to tell her about Rory."

"So you were a fucking coward?"

My head shoots up, rage coursing through my veins. "Coward? I'm the coward? That's rich coming from you, Dylan."

"Don't bring up my past, Griffin." He slams his hand on my desk. "I was a high school kid who didn't give a shit about the consequences of my actions. Eden was collateral damage. She's moved on. I have too. It's over."

I want to push back and ask him why he only fucks women who bear a striking resemblance to Eden. He's as stuck in his twisted past as I am in mine.

"You have a chance at something here, Griffin." He moves back in the chair. "Rory would want you to be happy. You know that. I know it."

Rory will forever be stuck in the same moment in time in my mind because of me.

It is all because of me.

"I made my choice." I fist my hands together on my desk. "Piper will move on. I will too. It's how it needs to be."

"You're telling me you're good with her meeting someone else? You have no problem with her fucking another man? Falling in love with him? That's all good for you?"

Every single word grates on my last nerve.

The thought of Piper with another man is more than I can bear.

I want her. Fuck I want a future with her but I can't. I don't get that. It's my price to pay.

"I made me choice," I repeat.

"What about her choice?" He stands and slams his hands on the top of my desk. "Why don't you let her make the choice for herself? Give her some credit, Griffin. The woman might love you as much as you love her."

"I didn't say I loved her, Dylan."

He huffs out a laugh. "You didn't have to."

***

"Did you set Marco up?" Morgan Tresoni waltzes into my office, unannounced.

I should fucking fire Joyce.

"No. I can't take any credit for that. Your soon to be ex-husband dug his own grave. He's the one who couldn't keep his hands off other people's stuff."

"He told me you almost killed him." She stands in front of my desk. "Is that true?"

"Almost is the operative word, Morgan. He's still a living, breathing piece of shit."

She laughs. "You've got that right."

"Did you come all the way down here to talk about Marco?" I stand. "You're almost free of him. The divorce will be finalized within the month."

"Good." She waves her left hand in the air. "I have a little something I need your help with."

I can't keep track of her engagement rings. "That's not the ring Marco gave you, is it?"

"No." She rolls her eyes. "This one is from Marty. You're going to love him, Griffin. He owns a hedge fund and a yacht."

I reach down to pick up a pad of paper and a pen. "One pre-nup coming up."

"You're the best, Griffin. You totally get how this marriage thing works."

I look at her. "Do you love Marty?"

"Sure." She shrugs. "I do."

"You're going to stick with this one through thick or thin, good or bad?" I cock a brow. "Better or for worse?"

"Look, I get that I haven't had the best luck when it comes to marriage." She eyes up her new engagement ring. "Just between you and me, I think I might have let Mr. Right slip through my fingers in college."

"How do you know he was Mr. Right?"

"He still owns this." Her hand leaps to the middle of her chest. "My heart."

I set the paper and pen back down. "Have you considered looking for Mr. Right, Morgan? Maybe you still own his heart too."

"I don't." Her voice softens. "I pushed him away. I didn't realize what I had until it was too late."

"Why did you push him away?"

She heaves a sigh. "I got scared. It felt like he was too good for me, and one day he'd wake up and realize it. I didn't want to be so far in that my heart wouldn't recover so I ended it first."

I search her face. "You regret that now, don't you?"

"More than you know, Griffin. More than you know."

Chapter 49

Piper

"His name was Rory."

I turn at the sound of Griffin's voice behind me. I've just exited my apartment on my way to the store. It's been weeks since I've seen him.

I've wanted to reach out to him numerous times, but I always stopped myself. Sebastian gave me the strength to do that.

He came into the gallery a week after we were both ordered out of Griffin's apartment. He brought me a gift. It was a painting by the same artist who had created the masterpieces that hang in Griffin's home office.

The artist is Rory Kent, Griffin's late brother.

I didn't press for more details than that.

I wanted to hear the story from Griffin when he was ready.

"Do you want to come in?" I touch the door of my apartment. "We can talk inside."

He nods as he approaches. "I'm sorry, Piper."

"I know," I say quietly as I open the door.

He follows me through in silence, closing and locking the door behind us. "I've spent all this time trying to come up with the right words."

I move toward the sofa, tossing my keys and my purse on an armchair. "They don't have to be the right words. They just need to be honest."

He waits for me to take a seat before he settles in beside me.

I reach to grab his hands and pull them into my lap. I finally look right at him. A light beard covers his jaw and his hair is in desperate need of a trim. He's not wearing a suit and tie today even though it's Tuesday morning.

Today, he's dressed much like I am, in jeans and a T-shirt.

"My brother Rory painted those pictures you saw at my place." His hands shake. "He was only seventeen when he created most of them."

"Seventeen," I repeat back. "They're incredible."

He nods sullenly. "He was like you. He wanted to be an artist. It was his dream."

Was…the word that distinguishes promise from loss.

"He died." His voice quakes. "Suicide."

I lower my head when the rush of tears hit me. "I'm so sorry."

I hear his swallow. "He hung himself in the bedroom of my parents' house in Connecticut."

"I can't imagine how hard that must have been for your family."

"We all died in a sense that day." He reaches for my hand and I grab tightly to him. "My dad disappeared into himself, my brother Draven fought through bitter anger. He still does."

I start to ask about him, but he squeezes my hand.

"My mom was broken," he goes on. "Rory was her baby."

"Losing a child must be devastating," I offer. "Losing a brother as well."

He looks at me with tears in his eyes. "We fought that day."

I struggle to control a sob. It's guilt. That's what has wrapped itself so tightly around his heart. He feels guilt over his brother's death.

"He had been accepted to an art school out in Los Angeles." He shakes his head. "Some prestigious place that only takes the brightest and best."

Conrad School of the Arts. I'd applied there too. I didn't get in.

"He was so smart, so fucking smart and we wanted him to be a doctor."

I nod through a veil of tears.

He exhales roughly. "That morning I told him that art would never be enough. I insisted he apply to Harvard or Yale. I told him to his face that if he didn't follow a more traditional path that he'd always regret it."

"You were trying to steer him in the direction you thought was best," I say quietly.

"I wanted the best for him." He nods. "My dad too."

I move closer to him, pressing my body next to his. "You can't fault yourself for wanting the best for someone you love."

"He asked me point blank if I thought his paintings were any good. If I thought he'd ever see one in a museum or an exhibit."

I stare into his eyes, knowing the answer already. It's what tears this beautiful man apart every day of his life.

"I told him they were good, but not good enough."

"Griffin," I whisper his name as I rest my forehead against his. "It's not your fault."

"He was a soft soul." He catches a sob in his throat. "He looked up to me. He followed me around for years, wanting to be like me. That kid craved my acceptance."

"You can't keep blaming yourself."

"After I left my parents' place that morning to drive back to the city, he called me." He presses his cheek to mine. "I didn't give him a chance to say a word. I just railed on him about expectations and responsibilities."

He drops his head down. "He was gone a few hours later."

I reach for his face and cradle it in my palms. "He didn't die because of you, Griffin."

Tears streak his cheeks. "He did, Piper. If I had understood the depth of his talent back then, I would have paid for art school. I had no idea."

"How could you have known?"

"I thought it was a frivolous choice. He kept those paintings hidden in his room." He exhales roughly. "My mom was the only one behind him and I drowned out her voice."

"His paintings are intense." I look at him. "There is so much pain in them. He was a tortured soul, Griffin."

"Sebastian and Dylan have said the same thing."

"Sometimes an artist uses their medium as a catalyst for their pain. I believe your brother did that."

229

I blow out a breath. "He put everything he was feeling into each stroke of his brush. He captured his internal struggles on canvas."

He nods in silence.

"Whatever drove him to take his own life was much bigger than what you two argued about." I feel a tear well in the corner of my eye. "He was in pain for a long time, Griffin."

"I wish I would have understood this when he was alive." He searches my eyes. "To my family, they were just paintings. We couldn't see beneath their surface."

"He was brilliant." I rest my head on his shoulder. "I'm in awe of what he created."

"I want to show you more of his work." He strokes my hair. "I want to tell you more about him."

Reaching up, I take his hand in mine. "I'd love that."

Chapter 50

Griffin

My intention wasn't to make love to her when I came to her place, but that's exactly what happened. We spent hours in her bed, sharing slow sensual kisses and a hard fuck that shook the walls.

I need her. She feels it now, but that's not enough.

"Piper." I trail kisses over her bare collarbone. "Wake up, baby."

Her eyelids flutter open. "I'm awake."

"I love you," I say the three words that have consumed me for weeks.

Her bottom lip quivers. "I love you too."

"You're the most incredible woman I've ever met." I rest my head on the pillow so I can gaze into her eyes. "You understand me in a way no one ever has."

"That's because I love you." She smiles softly. "I think I fell in love with you that first day in your office when I turned around and saw you."

I laugh. "It was love at first sight."

"Love at first beat of my heart after your eyes locked on mine."

"You felt that too?" I question with a quirk of my brow. "My heart beat harder after I saw you. Something changed. I knew you were meant to be a part of my life."

"Does that mean we have to thank Marco?" She scrunches her face. "I can't say the bad sex was worth it because I found you. It wasn't."

"He was bad in bed?"

She laughs. "He was a bad kisser. You do the math."

I kiss her. It's deep and lush. "I'm the best kisser, aren't I?"

"You're the best everything." Her hand jumps to my cheek.

"Where do we go from here?" I want to ask her to move in with me. Hell, I want to drop to one knee and make this woman my wife, but I need to take a minute and let this love thing sink in.

Her lips find mine again. "Boston."

"Boston?" I huff out a laugh. "What the hell is in Boston?"

She hesitates, her eyes jumping back and forth between mine. "I want something, Griffin. I want it for you and your mom. I know I haven't met her, but there's a picture of her in your home office, isn't there? That black and white photo of the woman in the silver frame?"

'That's my mom." I nod. "I want you to meet her Piper. I'll take you to meet her."

"Bring her to Boston."

"What the fuck is in Boston?" I smile.

"It's an art showcase hosted by Beck. It's a pretty big deal." She moves until she's almost sitting. "I was offered six placements in it, but I want the world to see Rory's work."

I follow her lead and lean back against the headboard. "What are you saying?"

"Let me talk to Beck, but I know he'll agree. Let's give Rory's work an audience." She rubs her chest. "My heart is so full right now."

"Slow down, baby." I reach over to cover her hand with mine. "I'm not following."

"I want to give three of my placements to Rory…to you." She squeezes my hand. "Your mom and you should pick out three of his paintings to display."

"You'd do that for him?" I feel a rush of emotion again. Fuck. I haven't cried this much since the day we lost my brother. I haven't allowed myself to feel.

She moves to wipe a tear from my cheek. "We're going to do that for him."

"Did I already tell you how much I love you?"

Her lips trail over my cheek to my mouth. "Show me, Griffin."

I do. I slide down her body, licking a path over her breasts until I settle between them. "This is my forever, baby. This is right where I belong. Inside your heart."

"Forever?" Her voice is barely a whisper. "You feel it too."

She nods. "I do."

"Every tomorrow is going to be better than the last, isn't it?" I kiss her nipple. "This is just our beginning?"

Her hand finds its way to my hair, tugging at the dark strands. "Every tomorrow, Griffin."

I slide lower, savoring the taste of her flesh until I reach her mound.

When my tongue flicks over her clit, she cries out. It's a sound that I'll crave every day of my life.

"I want you inside of me," she purrs.

"Let me have this first." I lick her slowly. "Give me this and then I'll make love to you."

"Make love," she echoes softly.

"To my future wife," I whisper under my breath.

I'm going to make it happen.

Forever isn't long enough for the two of us.

Epilogue

6 Months Later

Piper

"Both of my evening classes are full." I point at the calendar that Bridget printed out. "I don't see why I can't take over your Saturday spot."

She rubs her growing belly. "Tamara doesn't arrive for another two months so that's going to work out perfectly. I'll finish up my class, and you can launch another human form class in that spot if you want."

Of course I want to.

Teaching has become my lifeblood, next to loving Griffin.

The showcase in Boston was a huge success. I was offered an artist in resident placement in Italy, but the thought of leaving the gallery and my students behind didn't excite me.

A year ago I would have jumped at the chance to study abroad, but my priorities have changed.

I belong here at Grant Gallery, guiding people to hone their love of art.

My work with Beck on creating a show of Rory's pieces for a museum in Los Angeles has become a focus for me too. It's a labor of love for Griffin, his mom Val, and me.

His brother has checked in on it a time or two, but his pain over Rory's death is still too much.

It's been eight years, but grief is a personal journey and one that Draven is still trying to navigate.

"You should get home." Bridget shoves my purse toward me. "I don't need you here right now."

She's rarely in during the afternoons, but she dropped in today to discuss her maternity leave. I'll be taking over the day-to-day operations of the gallery while she takes a few months off.

I doubt like hell that she'll be out that long. She loves this place as much as I do and her baby daughter already has a crib set up in the office for her future visits.

"I don't clock out for another hour." I point at my watch. "Why don't you go home and see the boys and Dane?"

"They're going to a movie." She shrugs. "I'll stick around. You take off."

I don't argue. Griffin is working from home today. I kissed him goodbye before I came to the gallery earlier. He was in the middle of a conference call, but he still made time to tell me he loves me.

"I'll see you tomorrow?"

"You know it." A wide smile crosses her lips. "Have a good night, Piper."

"I will."

She nods briskly. "Oh, I know you will."

***

I turn my key in the lock of the apartment that I share with Griffin. It was his apartment, but it's ours now.

I sublet my place to a woman who just moved to New York from New Mexico. She's starry-eyed and eager to take Manhattan by storm. When I introduced her to Jo, they hit it off immediately.

When I saw Jo at the diner yesterday, she told me her new neighbor has already found the man of her dreams.

I push on the heavy wooden door and step into the foyer.

I stop in place, shaking my head, unsure if what I'm seeing is real.

"Mom? Dad?" My voice breaks. "Are you here?"

They both rush toward me and tug me into their arms. I haven't seen them since I left Denver to move to New York. We talk online and share the occasional video chat, but this is the first time I've had the chance to hug them in months.

I do, tightly.

I wanted them at the showcase in Boston, but my dad's fear of flying kept them grounded in Colorado.

I pull back from our embrace to take off my coat and drop my purse on the table. "What's going on? Is something wrong?"

"Everything is right in our world." Griffin appears behind my parents. "I flew them here because I needed to ask them a question. I had to do that in person, Piper."

I choke out a breath when I see the small gift box in his palm.

"Oh, shit," I mutter under my breath.

"Piper," my mom scolds me the same way she always has when I swear.

Griffin reaches for me. "Baby, come here."

I take his hand and follow him to the middle of the room.

He's wearing the very same suit he was the first day I met him. I'm wearing a white dress we picked out together last week at the vintage shop near my old place.

When I tried it on he told me I took his breath away. He does that to me every single day.

"I couldn't ask for your parents' permission to marry you without meeting them first." He smiles over my shoulder to where my mom and dad are standing. "They said *yes*."

I nod. "I will too."

He laughs before he drops to one knee. "You came into my life when I needed you the most. You taught me about forgiveness, and regret. You showed me that love could heal and transform a person."

My hand darts to cover my mouth.

"I love you with every part of who I am, Piper. Marry me. Just marry me and make me the happiest man on this earth."

"Yes." I bounce in my heels. "You know it's a yes."

When he opens the box and I see the ring, I can't control the tears. It's beautiful. It's a silver band with two stones; one diamond for his heart and one for mine. He's been telling me for months that he wanted to design the ring himself.

"It's perfect, Griffin," I whisper as he slides it on my finger. "This is perfect."

"Every tomorrow will be too." He stands to kiss me. "I'll make sure of it."

I will too. This man's happiness is what my dreams are made of.

"So…" My dad interrupts just as Griffin is about to brush his lips over mine. "Let's talk grandchildren."

Griffin's head falls back in laughter. I can't help but laugh too.

"Give us a minute to get married." Griffin smiles at my dad. "Let me have her to myself for a year or two and then we'll make you a grandpa."

"I can live with that." My dad steps back.

"I can too," I whisper to Griffin. "For now, all I want to do is love you."

His kiss says it all. We were meant to be together, our future is written and every tomorrow will be better than the day before.

Preview of WISH
A New Roommates to Lovers Standalone Novel

My twenty-fifth birthday was just like the twenty-four before it.

I stood next to my identical twin sister as we blew out the candles on our shared birthday cake.

She wished for a healthy new baby to add to the family she already has with her husband.

I wished for my parents to stop asking me why I wasn't more like my twin.

When I get back to Manhattan after my birthday trip, a surprise is waiting for me.

A tall, gorgeous, tattooed stranger is in my apartment.

Did I mention he's naked?

He says it's not a big deal. I say *it* is a BIG deal, if you know what I mean.

I assume he's there to see my roommate, but apparently I'm wrong since she left town while I was away.

Sebastian Wolf i*s* my new roommate.

I'm tempted to throw him out after the first day, but I agree to give him another chance.

When I start to wish for more, I discover that my new roommate isn't the man I thought he was.

Chapter 1

Tilly

I can't look away.

I know that I should. I realize that it's the right thing to do, but my gaze stays locked on the sight that's in front of me.

It's an intricate tattoo that covers the broad left shoulder of a man. The sharp lines of dark ink dip down to curl around his muscular bicep.

The ink on his skin isn't the only mesmerizing thing about him. This man is not only tall and dangerously good-looking, but he's hung. As in, the-largest-cock-I've-ever-seen hung.

The stranger in my apartment isn't wearing any clothes. He's completely naked and standing next to the now dead bouquet of flowers that were delivered to me before I boarded a flight to San Francisco five days ago.

His eyes are closed, his phone is in his hand, ear buds are tucked in place, and he's swaying slowly to what must be music I can't hear.

I should walk over to him and tap him on the shoulder, but I can't.

My feet have been planted in this spot, just inside the foyer of my apartment since I got home a few minutes ago.

My roommate, Lisa, wasn't expecting me home for another three days.

We don't keep in touch when one of us is out of town. We barely speak when we pass each other in the hallway.

Lisa and I are not friends.

We're roommates; nothing more and nothing less.

She has every right to invite a guy over. We only have one unspoken rule. I don't knock if her bedroom door is closed, and she does the same if mine is shut.

This is the first time I've ever caught a glimpse of one of the men she's sleeping with. It was worth the wait. This man is ridiculously hot.

I have to cross the room so I can get to the hallway that leads to my bedroom. I need to do that without the naked stranger noticing me. The last thing I want is to make small talk with Lisa's lover right now.

I finally pull my gaze away from him to look down at the hardwood floors. I need to think. I know the sight of Lisa's latest is jumbling my thought process. It's understandable though. Who wouldn't have trouble focusing when an incredibly attractive naked man is across the room?

"Matilda?"

I close my eyes when I hear the distinctive rumble of a deep voice. Why does this man's voice have to sound so damn sexy?

I've never corrected Lisa about my name. Matilda Jean Baker is my full name so my lawyer used it for the rental agreement I had her sign before she moved in. Almost everyone, other than my boss, calls me Tilly.

I admit I like that the naked stranger is calling me Matilda, although I'm shocked Lisa bothered to mention me to him.

My eyes open and I try to focus on the phone in my hand. It's a stall tactic. I'm hesitant to look up again. I've already got a mental image of his body. I doubt I'll ever forget it.

"I'm not supposed to be here," I say with a sigh. "I came home early."

I hear his footsteps as he nears me.

Dammit. The naked stranger is almost right in front of me.

"I thought you were supposed to be in San Francisco until Sunday."

I eye his bare feet. I know eventually I need to look up, but he's so close now and I don't trust myself not to stare at his dick. From this vantage point, I'll be able to see every vein and how wide the crown is.

"Matilda, are you okay? You're trembling." His hand brushes against my shoulder. "It's freezing outside. Did you come from the airport dressed like that?"

He's one to talk. At least I'm wearing clothes. The ripped jeans and old red college T-shirt I'm wearing did nothing to protect me from the winter weather that arrived while I was gone. When I left last week, it was forty degrees warmer than it is now.

"I'll make some coffee."

My head darts up when he makes that announcement. Who offers to make a pot of coffee at two a.m. when they're wearing nothing and their lover is probably waiting in her bedroom for another round.

My gaze skims over his smooth chest until it lands on the fur blanket he's wrapped around his waist. His left hand is resting on his hip, the blanket's edges bunched into his fist.

"I didn't startle you, did I?" He looks down and into my blue eyes. "It's dark in here. You probably didn't even notice I was standing over there until I said your name."

It's not that dark.

He's unaware that I was staring at him when I first walked in. That means I won't have to awkwardly try and explain to my roommate why I was checking out her nude lover.

At least now he's grabbed the fur blanket from where it's usually placed over the back of the brown leather couch. I use that blanket to wrap around myself when I watch my favorite shows in the evening. Now, I'll always think about the fact that it touched his naked body.

I shake that thought from my head. "I should get to bed. It's been a long day for me."

He nods. "I understand. There's nothing better than sleeping in your own bed after a trip."

I reach to pick up my suitcase before I head toward my bedroom. He's wrong. The only thing better than sleeping in my bed after my trip to San Francisco would be sleeping next to him. Although, after seeing him naked, sleep would be the last thing I'd want to do.

"It's been a pleasure meeting you, Matilda," he calls from behind me.

The pleasure is all mine. It's technically all Lisa's. She's the one who gets to enjoy what I just saw.

With any luck, I won't hear the two of them together. After the week I just had, the last thing I need is a reminder that there are men in the world who know how to a fuck a woman raw.

I have no doubt that the naked stranger in my living room is one of them.

Coming Soon

Preview of VERSUS
A New Enemies to Lovers Standalone Novel

I chose the woman I brought home with me last night for one reason and one reason only.

She looks like *her*.

It's the same with every woman I bring home with me.

They always look like *her*.

Light brown hair, sky blue eyes and a body that takes me to that place I crave. It's where I forget – *her* innocence, my cruelty, everything.

Last night was different.

This one didn't only look like *her*, she danced like *her*, spoke in a soft voice like *her,* and when she lost control on my sheets in that split second I live for, she made a sound that cracked my heart open. My heart; cold and jaded as it is, it felt a beat of something for this one.

She left before I woke up.

I need to forget about the woman from last night, just like I've forgotten every woman but the one who started me on this path to self-destruction.

I might have been able to if I wasn't standing in a crowded courtroom ready to take on the most important case of my career staring at the woman who crawled out of my arms just hours ago and into the role of opposing counsel.

I may be a high-profile lawyer, but her name is one I'd recognize anywhere.

The woman I screwed last night is the same one I screwed over in high school.

Court is now in session, and it's me versus *her*.

Chapter 1

Dylan

The world within Manhattan is its own beast. You learn that when you live here. When you claw your way around this city looking for something that's elusive.

For some, that's a job that will actually keep a roof over their heads.

For others, it's a relationship that will stand the test of time and weather the winds of change.

I have the first and no interest in the second.

My needle in the haystack is a particular type of woman.

I don't bother with blondes.

My cock has zero interest in redheads.

For me, it's all about the type of woman I see in front of me now.

Petite, light brown hair, blue eyes and a body that can move to the beat of the music.

Experience has taught me that if a woman can dance, she can fuck.

The woman I'm watching now is graceful, beautiful and within the hour will be in my bed.

I slide off the bar stool and approach her.

"I'm Dylan."

She taps her ear. "What was that?"

I lean in closer as she dances around me. "I'm Dylan, and you are?"

"Dancing." She breathes on a small laugh. "It's nice to meet you, Dylan."

"You've been watching me." I stand in place while the patrons of this club dance around me, brushing against my expensive, imported suit.

She spins before she slows. "I could say the same for you."

I look down at her face.

Jesus, she's striking. Her eyes are a shade of blue, that particular shade of blue that always takes my breath away.

"We're leaving together tonight."

She cocks one of her perfectly arched brows. "You're assuming that I'm not leaving with someone else."

"You're here alone." I spin when she does to catch her gaze again.

The skirt of her black dress picks up with the motion revealing a beautiful set of legs. "Maybe I like being alone."

"Not tonight." I reach for her hand.

She slows before she slides her palm against mine. "Dance with me, Dylan."

I breathe out on a heavy sigh. I haven't heard those four words in years. I haven't danced in as long.

I pull her close to me, sliding my free hand down her back. "What's your name?"

"Does it matter?" She looks up at me.

It never does.

I dance her closer to an alcove, a spot where the crowd is thin and the music quieter.

Her body follows mine instinctively, our shared movements drawing the admiring glances of others.

She's letting me lead now, but the sureness of her steps promises aggression in bed.

"We're wasting time. "

Her lips curve up into a smile. "Foreplay comes in many forms."

"Is that what this is?" I laugh. "I want to fuck you."

She presses every inch of her body against me. "You will."

My cock swells with those words. "Now."

"Patience, Dylan." Her lips brush my jawline. "I promise this will be a night you'll never forget."

Coming Soon

THANK YOU

Thank you for purchasing my book. I can't even begin to put to words what it means to me. If you enjoyed it, please remember to write a review for it. Let me know your thoughts! I want to keep my readers happy.

For more information on new series and standalones, please visit my website, www.deborahbladon.com. There are book trailers and other goodies to check out.

If you want to chat with me personally, please LIKE my page on Facebook. I love connecting with all of my readers because without you, none of this would be possible.
www.facebook.com/authordeborahbladon

Thank you, for everything.

ABOUT THE AUTHOR

Deborah Bladon has never read a romance hero she didn't like. Her love for romance novels began when she was old enough to board the bus, library card in hand to check out the newest Harlequin paperbacks. She's a Canadian by heart, and by passport, but you can often spot her in New York City sipping a latte and looking for inspiration for her next story. Manhattan is definitely her second home.

She cherishes her family and believes that each day is a gift for writing, for reading, and for loving.

Printed in Poland
by Amazon Fulfillment
Poland Sp. z o.o., Wrocław